I0530764

Abbreviated Epics

**Third Flatiron Anthologies
Volume 3, Fall/Winter 2014**

**Edited by Juliana Rew
Cover Art by Keely Rew**

Abbreviated Epics
Third Flatiron Anthologies
Volume 3, Fall/Winter 2014

Published by Third Flatiron Publishing
Juliana Rew, Editor

Discover other titles by Third Flatiron:

(1) Over the Brink: Tales of Environmental Disaster

(2) A High Shrill Thump: War Stories

(3) Origins: Colliding Causalities

(4) Universe Horribilis

(5) Playing with Fire

(6) Lost Worlds, Retraced

(7) Redshifted: Martian Stories

(8) Astronomical Odds

(9) Master Minds

License Notes

www.thirdflatiron.com

4

Contents

Editor's Note by Juliana Rew 7

Blade Between Oni and Hare by Siobhan Gallagher 9

HMS Invisible and the Halifax Slaver by Iain Ishbel .. 19

Beyond the Turning Orrery by Deborah Walker 31

Heart-Shaped by Manuel Royal 41

A Wolf Is Made by Jordan Ashley Moore 51

Through an Ocular, Darkly by Martin Clark 59

Damfino Plays for Table Stakes by Ben Solomon 71

Grins and Gurgles (flash humor): The Committee
    by Margarita Tenser 79

Rain over Lesser Boso by Gustavo Bondoni 85

The Perfection of the Steam-Powered Armour
    by Adria Laycraft 95

Assault on the Summit by Daniel Coble 105

Fortunate Son by Steve Coate 117

Odin on the Tree by Jo Walton 123

Refusing the Call by Elliotte Rusty Harold 127

The Blue Cup by Marissa James 133

Toward the Back by Jake Teeny 141

The Lost Children by Alison McBain 155

Great Light's Daughters by Patricia S. Bowne 165

Qinggong Ji by Stephen D. Rogers 171

On a Train With a Coyote Ghost
    by Robin Wyatt Dunn 179

Credits and Acknowledgments 191

*****～～～～*****

6

Editor's Note

by Juliana Rew

What is an epic? The dictionary defines it as a long poem, typically one derived from ancient oral tradition, narrating the deeds and adventures of heroic or legendary figures or the history of a nation. Third Flatiron's tenth quarterly anthology is a double issue, encompassing 19 very short stories on epical themes, such as swashbuckles and sorcery, alternate history and steampunk, megalomania, Frankenstein-type tales, and creation myths. As you might guess, it is a fantasy-heavy collection.

In reading submissions we were intrigued to receive a number of tales drawing upon Japanese and Chinese mythology. Our lead story, "Blade Between Oni and Hare," by Siobhan Gallagher, brings a marvelous— and often strange to Western eyes— viewpoint to the idea of an epic struggle. Other notable tales with feminine heroines include "Rain over Lesser Boso" by Gustavo Bondoni, "The Perfection of the Steam-Powered Armour" by Adria Laycraft, and "Qinggong Ji" by Stephen D. Rogers. What could be more appropriate than a manga-style cover?

If Victorian and Napoleonic steampunk is more your cup of tea, you'll find some damn fine exemplars in "Beyond the Turning Orrery" by Deborah Walker and "Through an Ocular, Darkly" by Martin Clark. Daniel Coble rounds out this group with a tale about a lost Himalayan expedition, "Assault on the Summit."

During my studies of medieval literature, I grew especially fond of the Norse sagas, both owing to their bloodthirsty, ambitious characters and strong moral content. We're happy to include Jordan Ashley Moore's "A Wolf Is Made," and Steve Coate's "Fortunate Son," passionate, and sometimes heartbreaking, stories inspired by the Viking civilization. And since epics by definition are poems, we've included a reprint of "Odin on the Tree" by poet/novelist Jo Walton.

Many writers are familiar with American mythologist Joseph Campbell's deconstruction of "The Hero's Journey," which outlines the basic pattern of an epic. We were tickled to see satirical pieces by Elliotte Rusty Harold and Jake Teeny, "Refusing the Call" and "Toward the Back." And Manuel Royal points out that sometimes the battle just goes "Heart-Shaped."

Our flash humor offerings, "The Committee," by Margarita Tenser, and "Damfino Plays for Table Stakes" by Ben Solomon, show us not to press our luck.

In "The Lost Children," Alison McBain provides a disturbing new take on the ancient Greek myth of the Minotaur, while Patricia S. Bowne invents a shiny new myth in "Great Light's Daughters." "The Blue Cup," by Marissa James, asks whether it is possible to recapture a long-ago, magical time.

While we don't have room for sweeping histories like "Dr. Zhivago," we call to your attention "On a Train With a Coyote Ghost" by Robin Wyatt Dunn and "HMS Invisible and the Halifax Slaver" by Iain Ishbel. These are affecting and luminous stories about the courage it takes to fight evil, fascism, and slavery.

"Abbreviated Epics" proudly showcases an international group of new and established speculative fiction authors, who share with us just a smidgen of the heroic and grand.

Blade Between Oni and Hare

by Siobhan Gallagher

Three days. Three days on a damn dead squid. Sun crisping her exposed skin, while the rest of her was soaked to the bone; tired of looking at the endless ocean, tired of holding her *katana* over her head, tired of her growling stomach and thirsty throat. Damn, that *umibōzu,* had nothing better to do than to go ship-wrecking. Oh sure, the sailors whined and begged on the deck, while she had the brains to grab her things and jump off, before the *umibōzu's* snaky limbs came crashing down.

But it wasn't the *umibōzu* they had to worry about in the deep waters.

The ship's sinking had stirred creatures from the bottom of the ocean, and they bubbled up, mouths wide and full of razor teeth. Yet it was the squid's misfortune to pick on a samurai—well, a rogue samurai. Though she had to give credit to her chest-eye, which saw the squid underwater as clear as a sunny day on land. As far as Kazuko could tell, she was the only survivor.

The scar tissue around the fist-sized chest-eye scrunched up every time spray hit it; she felt the chest-eye strain its sight, searching for a speck of land. It was hopeless. She drained her gourd of its last drops (irritating her thirst more than satisfying it) and tossed it into the ocean. How long 'til dehydration fully set in, before she became delirious enough to drown herself?

The squid corpse dipped a little, jerked in a steady direction; something probably had snagged one of the tentacles. The eye withdrew deeper into her chest, like it had when the *umibōzu* attacked—which made her

9

nervous. She didn't have the strength to fight off another abominable creature from the depths.

Kazuko clutched her *katana*, hands tense and wanting a fight. The jerking became a strong pull, waters swirling around her—a maelstrom! Sucked down, down into the whirlpool's mouth, spinning faster and faster, head-blind, nauseous. All she could do was dig her fingers into squid flesh, anchoring herself, and pray.

Though she knew the gods had abandoned her long ago, she had hoped that her end wouldn't be a watery grave.

The squid corpse rocked, lost momentum. Walls of water collapsed, briefly submerged her, spat her back onto the ocean surface. While her own eyes squeezed shut, the eye saw an island. The current pushed them toward it. An island populated by trees and scrubs, not a single hut on the coast.

As soon as Kazuko touched sand, she tumbled off and dry-heaved. She scraped soggy bangs out of her face and crawled up the beach to collapse on dry sand. No— she resisted rest—not yet. Her sword came first.

It took a full minute to stand; her legs badly wanted to give out. With all this vegetation, there had to be fresh water somewhere. The blade needed a good rinse before corrosion set in. She'd slept with a swordsmith, one of the best in Kyoto, and had threatened to tell his wife, to get this sword. Doubtful she could get away with that again—not with the eye, not now. So she had to take every care to maintain the blade.

She trudged into the thicket of trees, shade relieving her of the sun's harsh rays. Vines dripped from the branches, slick with sap and clung to her clothing. She ripped one from her shoulder, stirring the branches above. A series of snaps— *sploosh!* splattered onto her. A melon lay broken at her feet; bright orange on the outside, blood red on the inside.

What kind of melon was this? And for that matter, when did melons grow on trees?

Black seeds squirmed in the pulp. Her stomach clenched. She didn't trust her food unless it was dead still. She kicked the shards aside and moved on, listening for the trickle of water.

A stream was nearby, small, shallow, crowded by grass. The stones of the streambed appeared too perfectly set, as though arranged that way. But she pushed the idea away, unsheathed her *katana*, and rinsed it. She used a fistful of grass to wipe it dry, then repeated the process with the *kaiken* hidden in the sash of her kimono jacket.

She took a long gulp—oh, so sweet on her parched throat!—before exhaustion finally took her.

…

Rustling, soft paws, a flash of white.

The eye swiveled, lens stretched wide. A white hare was digging a mere two steps from her unconscious body. Her brain lurched out of slumber; her limbs were heavy, slow to move. The hare was still there, still digging. First the odd melon fruit, now a *white* hare?

Her stomach groaned, and suddenly, the color wasn't important. Only what it might taste like.

She lunged for the hare; it dashed out of reach by a fraction of a second. It hopped ahead, but not out of sight, as though waiting for her. Leading her.

Her hunger-addled mind spurred her into a chase. She threw whatever rocks came to hand, found a stick long enough to stab with, but even with the eye's precision, she couldn't land a killing blow. It was like the damn thing could *predict* her movements. And even when she stumbled, it would always wait for her to catch up.

Something wasn't right.

The hare ran straight into a cave. Ha, it was trapped! It was a dumb little animal, after all.

The eye didn't see anything within the cave's pitch blackness, so she entered, scraping through the narrow passage. Gooey threads slapped her face. She tore the goo away, found it wrapped around her hands. Eck! If she didn't know better, she'd say it was—

Chit, chit, chit.

Everything in her tensed. The *chit* came from above. From outside, the cave hadn't appeared large, but now the roof seemed *high* above the narrow space. Feeling less bold without her sword in her hand, she backed out.

The wind was knocked from her, followed by a high-pitched *hiss*. Movement in the dark, the eye only catching outlines. A giant spider leg impaled the ground, barely missing her foot. Another swipe, and its leg bristles snagged on her clothing. She wrenched away, tumbling over herself and into the sunlight. She scooted back, away from the cave's mouth. She glimpsed a silhouette—a human head and torso stuck onto a spider's thorax. It withdrew into the cave, out of sight.

Amaterasu's light, what was *that*?

Kazuko ripped the spider web from her hands—and was that. . . her throat tightened—blood? She picked at her trousers. No, just dried melon pulp. She flopped back, sighing. Stupid, to venture where she couldn't use her sword.

To add insult to injury, the white hare hopped out of the cave as if nothing was amiss.

...

Too tired to go hunting for a nuisance of a hare, Kazuko settled for the odd melon. It was that, or three-day-dead squid. She made a fire for the coming night, though it took a lot of kindling for the wood to finally catch. Strange wood, too. It burned more like coal and smelled of cherries and spices from foreign lands. She scraped the seeds into the fire, took a bite of melon. Watery, but not much flavor.

The hare was still there, watching her, just inside the eye's field of view. She tried not to think about it, the furry bastard. Though she would *love* to see it roasting on a spit.

...

In the morning, she set about collecting branches for a raft. The hare was of course there, keeping its distance.

"It won't work," said a chirpy voice.

She nearly dropped her bundle, looked around for the source.

"Here, down here. I believe you wanted to eat me yesterday." The hare hopped onto a boulder, to make itself more apparent.

Dammit, she knew there was something wrong with that melon. Should've never eaten it.

"You can't really be talking," she muttered.

The hare stood on its hind legs. "Why not?"

"Because you're—"

"A hare? Well, not just *any* hare. I'm a guardian of this island."

"Well, *guardian*," she said bitterly, "why won't what work?"

"It's obvious you're attempting to build a raft. But I'm afraid wood doesn't float here."

"We'll see."

Kazuko took an old log and marched with it toward the sea, with the hare following. At the beach, she tossed it into the waves—and watched it sink like a stone.

"The wood is much too dense," the hare explained.

She bit back a few choice words for the hare. "Fine. Then how am I supposed to get off this island?"

The hare moved close to the water, just out of reach of the waves, and thumped one hind leg on the sand. Awfully loud, coming from such a small creature. Moments later a scaly log popped up in the water—no wait, it was a crocodile.

"I'm friends with the crocodile," the hare said. "I can summon many to give you passage to the mainland."

There was something unsaid in the hare's words. Guardian or not, everyone had a price.

"What do you want in return?"

The hare looked up at her, nose twitching. "You have the reflexes of a warrior. So, warrior, I ask this favor: kill the *oni*."

"I haven't seen an *oni* here."

"Not yet. But I assure you he exists, in the deepest part of the island. He is a plague, and he is ruining the peace of this place."

She folded her arms, glanced over her shoulder in the direction of the cave. "I would think you'd rather have that spider-creature removed."

"No! Do not touch Shukujo Jorōgumo, she's of no importance to you. Kill the *oni,* and nothing more."

She'd made it mad. The little hare was standing tall, neck outstretched, chest puffed out. Rather amusing.

"All right, I'll do it."

"Excellent!" The hare returned to its unruffled state. "I'll show you the way."

…

They walked along the stream as it wound into the heart of the island. The stream widened in areas where the earth was barren, uprooted trees leaving deep depressions.

A crash, followed by a thunderous thump. Both Kazuko and the hare hid behind a large boulder. She put a hand on the hilt of her sword, peeked over the boulder. A red-skinned *oni,* twice the size of a hut, carried an armful of stones and dumped them by the stream. He plopped down, shaking the surrounding trees, and started arranging the stones.

"Doesn't look like a plague to me," Kazuko whispered.

"Well he is!" the hare squeaked. "And if you don't kill him, you'll never get off this island."

14

There the hare went, getting all huffy puffy again. She gave him a sardonic smile. "I said I would do it. Don't worry."

...

Admittedly slaying *oni* wasn't her specialty, but that just meant she had to get creative. Kazuko chopped down lengths of vines, tied the ends around adjacent trees. The hare had hopped away, not interested in how she handled the *oni,* only that she did it.

With the brush hiding the traps, all she needed was the *oni's* attention. She threw a rock at the *oni's* head. "Hey, you *yōkai* bastard!"

The *oni* scowled, tusks jutting out. He yanked a tree out of the ground, swung it for good measure, came for her as she retreated. *Snap-snap!* The *oni* fell face first, the impact shaking the ground.

Kazuko stumbled, caught her footing, and moved ahead to the next trap. Leaves, branches, twigs rushed at her, shoved her back into a tree. Splinters flew all around. Pain speared up her spine to coalesce into brief head-blindness.

She moved where the eye guided her, narrowly missing an entire tree as the *oni* struck the one behind her. She slashed at vines—a jagged rock swung down, smacking the *oni* square between the eyes. He roared, wild black hair standing on end. Oh, she had him now.

Or so she thought—before the vines seized her. The whole world went upside-down; legs bound, sword tip dragging on the ground. Gods, she hated magic forests.

The *oni* reached with a hand large enough to squeeze a cow. Quick stab—and he was howling in pain.

"Why would you do that, you stupid human-thing?" the *oni* said, through gritted teeth.

She took the opportunity to cut herself down, consequently plowing her head into the ground. The *oni* chuckled as Kazuko rubbed the bump on her noggin.

"'Human-thing'?" she spat back.

"I've never seen a human with an eye in their chest."

"A demon gave it to me—" she pulled her jacket over the eye. She wasn't a *thing*; she was human. . . with some extra abilities.

The *oni* sat on his haunches and leaned forward. "Interesting. So why have you come to hurt me?"

"It was a favor. . . for a hare."

"A white one? Why would you listen to a hare?"

"I—" She frowned. "Honestly don't know. It promised passage off this island if I killed you."

The *oni* snorted. "That was my brother, not a hare. He's tried this before, but with no success."

"Obviously," she muttered.

The *oni* glared at her, but went on, "He thinks with me dead, he will have a chance with Shukujo Jorōgumo."

"What do you mean?"

"She's my lover."

Kazuko almost gagged at that.

She stood, sword held low but ready if she needed it. "Look, I have no interest in your little love triangle, but I need a way off this island. Can you provide passage to the mainland?"

The *oni* shook his head. Her hand tensed on her sword.

"But if you slay me," he said, "Shukujo Jorōgumo will not let you off this island alive."

That certainly put the situation into a conundrum: either kill the *oni* and risk the wrath of Shukujo Jorōgumo, or stay on this forsaken island. Or. . . She looked up at the melons sprouting from the treetops.

. . .

"You did it!" The hare hopped onto the still chest of the *oni*. Sticky blood coated the *oni's* front; the hare stood on its hind legs and started dancing a jig. It suddenly shed its fur, revealing blackened skin; its long ears turned into yellow-stained horns.

16

"A guardian, huh?" She folded her arms, frowning at the imp.

He looked up at her with the same hare eyes, but they were cold, not like a hare's mild expression at all.

"I find people are more cooperative with a hare than a demon." His gaze fell upon her chest-eye. "Though I suppose with a soul as black as yours, that wasn't necessary. But wasn't it fun?"

Her chest-eye rolled. Exasperated, she thought: Oh yes, always fun to do someone else's bidding. Like I'm a damn servant.

"Now for your side of the bargain." She gestured east, toward the mainland.

On the beach, the imp did his thump-summon, and a row of crocodiles bobbed to the surface, all lined up. Cautiously, she stepped onto the first one, ready to jump off if she had to. The crocodile didn't seem to mind, or even notice.

"Well, go on now. I want to be alone with my new bride."

She hid her smile, moved to the next croc and the next. It was like walking on stepping stones. The crocs behind her moved up to continue the path, one by one. It would be a long walk to the mainland.

All the better, for in the distance behind her, she heard the *oni's* roar and the imp's unhappy squeaks.

About the Author

Siobhan Gallagher is a wannabe zombie slayer, currently residing in south Texas. Her fiction has appeared in several publications, including AE - The Canadian Science Fiction Review, COSMOS Online, Abyss & Apex, and Unidentified Funny Objects anthology.

Occasionally, Siobhan does this weird thing called "blogging" at: defconcanwrite.blogspot.com

This story was inspired by the Japanese fable, "White Hare of Inaba."

*****~~~~~*****

HMS Invisible and the Halifax Slaver

by Iain Ishbel

The setting sun emerged from the low clouds, and, like magic, the Atlantic turned from sullen grey to copper. "Deck there, a ship! Schooner, sir, broad on the starboard quarter." *Exactly* like magic, thought Lieutenant Mitchell. . . and not for the first time.

"Starboard your helm," he ordered. "Enchanter to the quarterdeck!"

In the fading evening airs His Majesty's Ship *Invisible* began a sluggish turn. A portly body arrived at Mitchell's side.

"What ship is it?" asked John Samphire, master enchanter.

"We don't know yet, Mr. Samphire, but this'll be why we're here. Tell me what you can."

Samphire raised his arms, uttered a quick prayer to Hecate, and began an enchantment. Mitchell's neck tingled, and he composed his expression carefully.

"Dead ahead now, sir!" called the masthead hand.

"Let go and haul!"

The crew snubbed the lines, and the little ship settled on a new course, just as Mr. Archibald the master arrived upon the quarterdeck. He had not been sent for, nor was it his watch, but his sailing skills were unsurpassed. "Mr. Archibald, conduct the ship please." Already the sun was dipping below the horizon, and the light was fading fast. "Can we get up to 'em before dark?"

"Aye sir," said Archibald, and settled in by the wheel, frowning. "I don't think we'll manage before the wind goes, sir. They will be right downwind when it comes back, though. Sooner or later, we'll catch them."

Mitchell nodded, and turned to Samphire.

"Can't tell much," the enchanter said. "Roughly our size, but a fair bit lighter. Not moving much at all—that is to say, we're all moving in the current, but from the ocean's point of view, both ships are perfectly still."

Archibald rolled his eyes. The master belonged to one the Free Scots Churches, who held the doctrine that nothing born of Hecate could have value. Despite a decade's secret service with the King's Own, he had no time for enchanters or their impractical ways.

And sometimes, despite his own position, Lieutenant Mitchell knew exactly how the "Wee Frees" felt. He stifled a smile and climbed into the rigging.

...

At the masthead, Mitchell passed his expensive night-glass to the masthead lookout.

"How big d'you think, Gunn?" he asked. "The French have a fair range of schooners."

The man peered through the long telescope for a moment, unhurried by the presence of his commander. "Wouldn't like to say French, sir, Baltimore-style mebbe. Right wicked lines, mind you. Might be a slaver, sir."

"Right," said Mitchell, "We'll find out in the morning, then." He took back his glass and made to leave, but the lookout cleared his throat meaningly. "Yes, Gunn?"

"Not to be rude, sir, but couldn't Mr. Samphire whistle up a wind for us? Ship's enchanter must know how."

"Ah, we'd have 'em then, eh?" Mitchell chuckled, but shook his head. "First of all, whistling up a wind is damn'dly difficult. I'm no expert myself, mind, but it takes at least a dozen air 'chanters to whistle up any breeze you'd notice—and even then it doesn't last long."

"Long enough to catch a Yankee slaver, though, sir, maybe?"

"Well, maybe so. But Mr. Samphire couldn't enchant air anyhow. He's a water man, didn't you know?"

20

"Oh." Gunn's face fell, and he knocked on the wood of the mast three times He turned away and began scanning the horizon again. "Water enchanter, I'd forgotten that."

Mitchell sighed. Prejudice, it seemed, was not for Christians alone.

...

"American, Nicholas?' Samphire sat in a canvas chair, raising a leather-bound bundle of papers to a single lantern. The room smelled of cinnamon and dust. "Are you sure?"

"In point of fact, John, no. There was little enough to see of her sails without a wind. Gunn seems confident, though—American-built at least."

"Well, I'd trust a Navy topman. And up to no good?"

"Oh, quite so," Mitchell replied. "A fast schooner heading empty to Halifax? Meeting a French spy or some such, if you ask me."

"And yet we simply wait?"

Mitchell nodded ruefully. "Until the wind comes up, we cannot—"

Samphire lurched from his chair with a cry of pain.

"What in Hecate's name?" Mitchell was on his feet.

"It's the schooner—," gasped Samphire. His eyes were crushed shut, and his fists clenched the sides of his head. "O, the sound—"

"Surgeon's mate!" Mitchell knelt over Samphire, hands shaking. The enchanter was utterly white. Feet pounded above their heads.

Samphire opened his eyes slightly, though he kept his ears covered. "The worst is over, I think." The single surgeon's mate rushed into the room as Samphire sat up. "Don't trouble yourself, Pierce. I'll be all—"

21

"Pass the word for the commander!" A muffled cry from the deck above, and Mitchell found himself on his feet.

"John, I must—"

"I am quite well now, I promise. The pain has abated—attend to your duties, I beg of you."

Mitchell clapped his friend on the shoulder as he rushed out of his cabin. As he arrived on the quarterdeck, it was entirely dark, the deep absorbing blackness of a cloudy night at sea.

"Are we to have our wind, Mr. Archibald?"

"No sir, not a breeze, I swear it. Only, Mr. Samphire's enchantment—" Archibald gestured to the pieces of a shattered wooden ring, floating in a bowl of salt water. "That bloody schooner's moved away, somehow. We must've missed something. She's kedged off into a deep current, or caught a lucky land breeze. I'm awfy sorry, sir."

"Hecate's triple tits," swore Mitchell. And Archibald, despite his strict Presbyterian morals, simply nodded.

Samphire arrived on deck, still pale. "It's gone, isn't it?"

"*She* is," said Mitchell. "And what else do you know, Mr. Samphire?"

The enchanter's eyes were dark. He raised an arm and pointed. "I know it went that way. Does that help at all?"

Archibald raised his eyes to heaven. Mitchell, through herculean efforts, did not. "Very good, master enchanter, thank you. Mr. Archibald, when it is possible, set course for Halifax. Which is, of course, *that way.*"

...

The hills of Halifax rose above the harbour like the walls of a fortress, sullen in the morning rain. A dozen Royal Marines with a decent sergeant and a sober chaplain could hold the Citadel Hill fortress against any number of

Yankees—Micmacs or no Micmacs. And who held the fortress held the harbour. No wonder the colony had been unable to join the thirteen to the south when they'd rebelled.

In the sodden grey calm of dawn, Mitchell swept the harbour with his glass. An odd variety of ships here, so far from the ports of Europe. Fast Caribbean schooners, British ships of war, several privateers under the colony's distinctive pale flag. A single Spanish man o'war, small wooden cross flaming at the maintop. And a baker's dozen of American ships sprawled willy-nilly about the long harbour, brazenly flying their defiant Stars and Stripes.

Samphire muttered in the Old Language behind him. Mitchell's feet tingled with the enchantment, and he glanced hurriedly at Archibald, who like all Christians had not noticed a thing. "That ship is here," said Samphire, rolling a splinter of wood between his fingers. "It's the thin one, in shallow water by the rocky little island."

Mitchell let out a long, relieved breath, and raised his glass. "The *Belinda*," he said. "A clear slaver, that, and under an American flag." He frowned and looked more closely at her waterline. "She's been loaded."

"Good," said Samphire. Archibald and Mitchell both looked up in surprise. Samphire frowned. "Does that not mean we can take the ship, and free the poor slaves?"

"It does not," said Mitchell, and Archibald coughed. "We cannot condemn an American ship for following American laws, Mr. Samphire. D'you think we'd let that Spaniard take you away for the Inquisition?"

"Of course not, Nicholas, but slavery, surely—we are King's agents, after all. We must do more."

Mitchell looked grimly at the schooner's wicked lines and raked masts. "What do you suggest?"

Samphire looked about, then pointed to the stern davits. "Let us take that rowboat over to him."

Even looking at a cold-hearted slaver in the sleet rain of a dreary Halifax dawn, Mitchell could not contain a thin smile.

"Very well," he said. "Kindly call away the jolly boat, Mr. Archibald. Perhaps something will occur to us on the way."

...

They found no inspiration, and the pale, balding captain of the *Belinda* was coldly unsympathetic. "You'll stay clear, mister. This is an American ship, and you will not come aboard."

"I'm a King's officer," Mitchell tried. "When the wind comes up, I'll have a frigate over here before you can say 'Continental Congress.' What will you say to the Royal Marines?"

The American captain looked over his shoulder and made a gesture. "Be damned to you, King's man."

A naked, coal-black body flew over the rail, arms and legs flailing wildly, a line trailing from its neck. One hand grasped desperately at the broad knot—then with a horrible damp *crack* the hemp jerked taut. The man's legs kicked twice, and the dead body bounced off the hull.

Samphire spoke loudly, strange words from a dark book. The waxen bag was floating on the water nearby.

The four oarsmen covered their ears, grimacing.

"What are you doing?" asked Mitchell. Everyone around him was mad, quite mad. The slave was dead. His ears were roaring, and the *Belinda* seemed to be far away, down a dark tunnel.

"Nicholas!" Samphire hissed urgently. "I've the whole enchantment. What shall I do with it?"

Mitchell looked at his friend, his mind spinning. The portly enchanter's face was dark with blood, his eyes bulging. He was breathing in long, laboured gasps. "I shall burst, Nicholas—"

"Trap him," Mitchell blurted. "Lower the tide!" Samphire's eyes opened wide, and he nodded.

"My wind!" called the American captain. "Where is my wind?"

"It is not your wind," Samphire said loudly, "necromancer." He made a sharp twisting gesture, and all around rose a rushing noise. a thousand mill-streams opening all at once. The low tide began dropping even further. One of the oarsmen swore a dreadful oath in the Old Language.

"Death sorcery," Samphire continued, "knows no element." His voice rang in the wet air. "And that dead Negro's soul shall never bring you the wind you demanded. It has agreed to a water enchantment instead."

The *Belinda* touched bottom with a gentle crunching and toppled slowly onto her side. The jolly boat still floated, but not for much longer. Mitchell stepped out onto the sand. The water was barely to his knees, and still dropping. He sloshed toward the beached slaver.

"Tide," Samphire continued, "goes out quite happily. Today it has simply decided to go rather further out than usual."

A great moan issued from inside the schooner's hull, and she settled even further. A sailor jumped from the rigging down to the sand and began running toward the far shore.

Mitchell touched his fingers to the bare copper of the exposed bottom. He leaned sideways to look at the fallen ship's figurehead. It was an ugly piece of work: a bare-breasted Negress with her hands chained cruelly behind her, a rope around her throat. She lay helpless, pressed into the sand of Nova Scotia.

Mitchell stood straight. "Well," he said. "Well, now."

"Captain Joseph, sir?" A grizzled sailor called from the stern, his voice rough with the colony's unmistakable accent. "Them slaves has all shifted across sideways. Should I unchain 'em?"

The slaver captain himself stood crookedly on the side of the binnacle. "What in hell is happening?" he said, his voice high. Another of his crew dropped to the sand and ran.

Samphire made to step out of the jolly boat, then pulled his foot back in and sat on the gunwale instead. "It is simple enough," he said. "Rather than whistling up a wind with your necromancy, you've helped me send out the tide, and now you are all adrift here. Is that the term, Lieutenant?"

"It is 'aground,' Mr. Samphire, not 'adrift.' The *Belinda* has been careened aground here, as you say. Which means—**Mr.** Joseph is it?—you are ashore in His Majesty's colony of Nova Scotia. And there is no slavery permitted here."

Joseph roared with rage. "I'll kill them with my own hands before I let you—". Then he recoiled.

Mitchell's sword was loose in his hand. From the wet sands around him rose a nimbus of steam like a dark cloak. An amethyst throbbed dully on the saber's pommel, lighting the steam with a purple glow.

"Oh, dear," said Samphire from the jolly boat. "The King's enchantment."

Joseph's face was pale, but red around the mouth and eyes. "Sorcery, by Christ! You're no officer, you heathen bastard, no kind of gentleman!"

"You are mistaken," said Mitchell coldly. "I follow the Old Ways and am yet an officer of His Majesty. And whether I am a gentleman or no—if you commit murder, I shall hang you myself. I say this in the name of the King." The amethyst pulsed with purple light.

Joseph's lips moved as if to spit. He tugged out a broad cutlass and leapt down to the sand, took two heavy steps toward Mitchell, then more; running almost, with his cutlass rising.

Mitchell dropped into a crouch. His sabre was in *sixte*—after years of training his body fell *en garde* very naturally. He waited, toes pointed apart, body half-turned. Joseph was still moving forward, cutlass raised for a cruel slash.

"Surrender yourself," said Mitchell, "if you—"

As he spoke, Joseph lunged with a cry, slicing the heavy blade down toward Mitchell's head. Mitchell's blade swept up without thought, a roofline above his head. The cutlass clunked off the parry, a branch hitting the rooftop. Mitchell reflexively riposted, cutting toward the side of Joseph's unprotected head. His first conscious decision was to halt the blade. "In the King's name—put up your sword."

Joseph scrambled back, feet slipping on the wet sand. He was breathing heavily, and his eyes had a wild stare. "You're a damned Loyalist bastard, and you've no right. I'm a rich man, a godly man—"

He lurched forward, cutting at Mitchell's leg. Mitchell dropped the point of his sabre straight down to *prime*. The simple parry blocked Joseph's clumsy swipe— and this time Mitchell did not halt his riposte. His wrist whipped the blade straight upwards, no curve nor twisting, and its edge slid neatly beneath Joseph's chin. The little man simply fell, his graceless lunge now a simple collapse, face-first to the sand.

The last sight Mitchell had of his enemy was the bald top of his head. Already blood was staining his pale hair and the wet sand around his body.

Mitchell turned away with a strange sense of regret. "*Belinda*, there," he called. "Who's in command now?"

The grizzled crewman stepped down from the edge of the hatch. "Reckon that's me, my lord," he said tentatively. "Walsh, sir."

"Unchain those slaves, Walsh."

"Aye, aye, sir," the man replied, and licked his lips nervously. "Are you having them, sir?"

27

"Let 'em free, man. They can walk to the shore from here, and then you can try to right that ship of yours."

"Best hurry," Samphire called from the jolly boat. "Can't hold back the tide forever."

...

"They were interfering with the Underground Railroad, sir." The grey-haired leader of the freed slaves was walking with Mitchell on the stony beach below the little shelters. "Lord, all the way from South Carolina. Awful thing to be recaptured after all that distance."

"Well, what will your people do now?" asked Mitchell. After several silent steps, he turned to look at the freedman, who was staring ahead fixedly, his eyes glistening. "Here, are you quite well, Scipio?"

Scipio took in a shuddering breath. "Well enough, sir; only every few hours it comes over me again—*free,* sir. We all can do whatsoever we take to."

Mitchell felt a stinging in his own eyes and cleared his throat, glaring across the water to the bustle of Halifax. "Well, quite so," he said gruffly, "Quite so. I cannot tell you what to do, Scipio, but I will happily give you my advice, one man to another."

"What advice then, Mr. Mitchell, sir?"

"Were I you, I should make no promises, not to the Governor nor any man. You've got enough to live on for now, and your people can fish these waters freely. There's a whaling factory down the shore there. The men who own it are Quakers. They'll treat you fairly, and they respect good workers. But I'll not tell you what to do."

They had come finally to the *Invisible's* jolly boat, pulled up on the beach. The sailors were lying on the warm pebbles, basking in the sunlight and smoking. Samphire sat in the stern of the boat, reading a small dark volume. As Mitchell and Scipio approached, the sailors began to sit up and move toward the boat, stretching and yawning.

"You tell *them* what to do," Scipio observed.

"So I do," agreed Mitchell. "It's not a Christian's Paradise you've come to, after all. There's plenty wrong in the world yet, and we're fighting a war that may yet destroy us. Nova Scotia might not improve for a while, not even by the King's will." He frowned, looking down at his feet. "I don't even know if this has done any good."

"Well, sir, here's near two hundred of us who ain't slaves no more, Mr. Mitchell. That's one step closer to Paradise, and it's purely thanks to you." The freedman offered his hand, and the King's man took it.

"Well," said Mitchell, "That'll have to do for now."

About the Author

Iain Ishbel is a recovering high-school teacher who now prefers the quiet life of a professional writer on Canada's Pacific coast. He lives in a very small house with one rather small wife and two extremely small daughters. He loves them all very much, except the house.

*****~~~~~*****

Abbreviated Epics

Beyond the Turning Orrery

by Deborah Walker

"Know this, if there is one lesson to take from me. Know that sin is worse than the unwinding." I remember Maestro Iron Bars ending each lesson with those words. As boys, in the safety of our dorm we would mock him: "Remember, remember," we would say in portentous tones. But he was wise. I think even as children we knew it. That's why we tried to diminish the fearful meaning of his words with our jokes.

As I grew older, I began to understand. I have been a man concerned with sin. Sin corrodes. Sin obscures the savour of life. Sin shrinks the spirit and corrupts all that is good. I am now the monastery Maestro. I lead my brothers and the students though the pathway of faith. I counsel them to alleviate the sins that all men in our weakness commit.

I have made two sins worthy of note in my life. I am about to embark on the third. Here is the story of my first sin.

...

That night we sneaked out of the dormitory. We made our way through the still corridors and into the chapel. We stepped onto the ever-moving spiral stairs and entered the winding chambers, where the newly made waited for the Makers' touch.

"Come quickly, Geoffrey," said Dominique, as I stared at the blank face of the newly made. "We don't want to be caught."

"Every sane person is quiescent," I said. That was how I should have been as well. But I followed him. Oh, how I followed him.

"Here," he said, pointing to an unremarkable part on the wall. "When I press this. . . " His hands touched the

31

metal slats. The wall slid apart with a clattering noise, to show an unlit passageway.

"How did you find it?" I whispered.

"I looked. Come on." Dominique stepped into the tunnel and turned to me. I remember his eyes, lit like crystal blue stars.

We walked in silence (although the spring in my chest seemed to quiver at an unwholesome rate), until Dominique stopped. He asked, "What do you think of this?"

In the gloom was an immense metal doorway, embossed with script that I didn't recognise, although I was a student of some note in the forgotten languages. "Is this the way outside the city?" I ran my fingers over the unreadable scripts, metal curls of an unknown tongue.

"No." His voice was quiet, reverential. "This is the vault."

The vault! The unopened vault. Only the Maestro was allowed to know its location.

"Shall we go inside, Geoffrey?"

"No," I replied, startled at his suggestion.

He smiled. "I would like to go inside. And you would come with me, but I don't have the key. Let's move on."

The tunnels ended in a blank wall. "Watch carefully, Geoffrey." I nodded. The old metal slid apart. I breathed in the air of the outside for the first time in my life.

He held out his hand. "Don't be afraid."

"I'm not," I said. But I was, dreadfully afraid. But not for myself.

...

Outside the Tin City, the cogs that move the world are close to the surface. Outside you can hear the very turning of the machine.

Dominique led me to a patch of soft wire grass. We lay on our backs for a time, watching the planets moving smoothly along their celestial wires. The unnamed clusters of small blue stars weaved along their spiral pathways. The Copper Mother was prominent that night, gleaming in the full crystal moon. I could almost make out with my naked eye the mysterious canals that ran along her surface. The ruby twins were coming into ascension on either side of the Copper Mother. And the Hag was, as always, a distant glimmer, moving on a wire, many times the length of the worlds.

I said nothing, waiting for him to speak.

Eventually he said, "Nonsense. It's all nonsense." He glared at the night-sky as if he could change the dance of the heavens with the force of his will.

He'd been reprimanded by the Maestro that day. His initiate's thesis, "In Search of an Alternate Astrological Model," had been rejected.

Master Rilliams, the language tutor, had whispered to me, "I read it. It was near blasphemy. Stay away from that boy, Geoffrey."

"Dom should have been expelled," whispered the boys. "He would have been if he wasn't the son of the Master Clock Builder. . . "

"Do you have to be so intense all the time?" I asked. I never understood Dom's willingness to dismiss the beauty of the world. My head was throbbing with the constant click of the mainspring that wound the world which was so loud on the outside. (Outside. We were outside!) I picked a copper cricket out of the grass, and held it to my ears listening to the small tick of its tiny internal springs.

"If we're wound, who winds us?" asked Dom.

I touched his chest. "How can you deny that?" I thumped his chest a little harder. I was afraid for him, and that made me scared.

"I don't deny the fact, Geoffrey. I deny meanings. Who winds us?"

I sighed. "The Makers wind each creature, at the start of their life, determining their lifespans."

Dom stared at the sky. "Look at the Hag Star, Geoffrey. One day, perhaps within our lifetimes, she will be close, and then what will happen?"

What would happen was not in dispute. "The world will unwind, every creature will unwind. And the Makers will restart the world. As they have done many times before. This we know."

Dom frowned. "I have been thinking about Icantari, lately."

I laughed. My friend was a model for Icantari. He had the same pride, the same hubris, the same desire to reach beyond the boundaries the Makers set for us.

"Icantari flew beyond the lamp of the sky," said Dom.

I repeated the old legend, told to boys. It was not part of the Maestro's books. "Icantari met the Makers, and that was the start of the promise. That the Hag Star will come after a thousand years, and the world will unwind, but that the Makers will always rewind the world."

"Yes," said Dom.

"So?" I said. "It's a pretty story, that's all."

"But how did he get to beyond the stars?"

"In his magic ship. He left the Tin City and went to live with the wildings. He fell in love with the wilding king's daughter, and she gave him the secrets of the flight. And then he left her to fly to the Makers. He never came back. She died, her mainspring snapped in two. Very romantic. Very sad." I shrugged. I was a monastery initiate, and the concerns of women were not my concern.

"Do you think there's any truth in the story?" Dom asked.

"If it happened, it's all in the long gone past. The world has unwound a hundred times since then."

"Why can't we go beyond the sky, Geoffrey? Beyond the orrery of the planets, past the lamp of the sun.

34

Why is flight banned? I've dreamed of a machine that will take us to the Makers. That seems to me the ultimate expression of faith."

"Does it?" I asked, wondering if he could really believe that.

"I'm leaving."

There were so many things to say: Don't go. Don't leave me. The copper cricket fluttered within my hands. Life ticked on.

"You'd break your initiate's vows?" I asked. "You'll break your promise to the Makers?"

"You won't come with me, will you?"

I kissed him. It wasn't enough, but it was all I could think to do.

...

They didn't look for him very hard.

His father came to the school to listen to the explanations of Maestro Iron Bars. "It's good that I have other sons," I heard him say as he left.

Dominique became part of the boys' mythology, a story to be whispered at night to frighten your schoolmates. Dismantled by the wildings, who the boys earnestly believed roamed the outside, was the usual end to his tale.

My first sin was being party to Dominique's vow breaking. I should have reported him to the Maestro. They might have bought him back to the Tin City. He would have been safe, and he would have been with me. The words of the Maestro Iron Bars began to shape in my mind. I should have run straight to the Maestro. But I loved my friend too much for that.

...

And the second sin was greater, and it came to me late in my life, and this is how it occurred:

Years passed. My old masters wound down, their bodies recycled into children and placed in the chapel ready for the touch of the Masters. All my friends, too, until I found myself the eldest of my generation and was given the position of the Maestro. I always remembered Dominique and tried to be sympathetic to the students, remembering what it was like to be young and foolish, and to be blind to the sight of the Makers' hand on the spring.

...

He came to me when I had been Maestro for ten years, when the Hag Star rode bright in the sky. He came at night, when I was sitting at my desk in quiescence. He crawled through my open window. He was unlike the beautiful boy I remembered. His body was almost a ruin, although the tick within his mainspring was still vigorous. Wherever he had been, there had been no chance for regular maintenance. But I knew him.

"Hello Dominique," I said.

"Aren't you surprised to see me?"

"I've been expecting you all of my life." That was only partly true. My dreams in which he died equalled the dreams in which he lived. His eyes were still the same, still the crystal blue of the unnamed stars. "Where have you been, Dominique?"

"I've been building. On the outside there are others. Only a few, but they've helped me."

I grabbed the edge of the table. So the stories were true. The wildings lived outside the Tin City. I pitied them, living as they did outside the Masters' mercy. "You should have bought them to the city," I said.

"No. That would not have served them well. There are more things in the world, than you know, Geoffrey. There are stories outside your philosophies."

Blasphemy!

"Do you remember the story of Icantari, Geoffrey?"

"I do."

"Well then," he said with a smile, "you see him before you. I have built my flying machine. Shall I take you to see it?"

"No."

"It's extraordinary, Geoffrey. I believe that it will fly through the night sky to the Makers."

"No."

He grinned. "I thought that you'd say that. Do you regret not coming with me, Geoffrey?"

His words took me back. I, who had been faithful to the Makers, had taken no companion, never raised a new child. I, who had spent my unwindings in service, was transported back to the raw boy lying in the grass. "What use are regrets?"

"I have something for you," he said, placing a metal box on the table.

"What is it?"

"The key to the vault."

The vault? As Maestro I had visited that locked place many times.

"Shall we read the secrets together, Geoffrey?"

"No," I said. Despite his shabby appearance, I felt drawn to him. There was something about him. In all my life, only Dominique has tempted me from my vows to the Makers. Even now, in old age, I trembled in his presence. How can that be? It seemed a holy thing. That intense longing for another was surely something from the Makers. I shuddered—it was as if the Dismantler was at my shoulder, tempting me. Dominique wasn't for me, and he never was.

"You don't want to go inside the vault, Geoffrey? Then I'll take my findings to the people of the Tin City. I'll parade my flying machine in the streets. Let the people decide. The Hag grows bright in the sky. The world's unwinding is at hand. I think you will find that not all go willingly."

"I won't let you do that."

"No?" He opened the metal box and took out the key. "You won't be able to stop me."

He thought he knew me so well, but he only knew the boy I was. The authority of my life-time asserted itself, and although I knew that I loved him, I also knew that he was dangerous.

I called for the guards. They took him away. On my orders they dismantled him the next day.

But he left me the key. I kept it, as memory to the boy I had been, who I might have been. It was a reproach, something I could hardly understand; still, I kept it.

Maestro Iron Bars was right. Sin robs life of every joy, every contentment. The time of the Hag was at hand, and I should have served the Makers. I should have helped my brothers. For Dominique was right, not everyone faces the End of Days willingly. But I was silent. Sin wrapped me in its heavy cloak.

. . .

Some time passed, until the night my reverie was shattered as I rested in quiescence. For a moment I didn't understand.

"The main spring of the world is stopped!" I heard the frightened voices of men and boys. The cogs that turned the world became still, and a hush permeated the city. A monstrous silence.

I took the key and unlocked the vault. I read the stories in the forgotten languages. It confirmed the promise made to Icantari. The world that was unwound would always be renewed. It was not enough.

Why should the world unwind? As if the world was a switch. Switch on, switch off. Tick, tock. This was the way of things. This was the way of the Makers.

Except. . . I knew a boy who had a dream, and he had spent a lifetime making his dream. I walked, for the second time of my life, to the outside and found Dominique's ship waiting for me.

I was like a copper cricket, staring uncomprehending at the immense sky. I listened to the quiet tick of my life, winding down, all the time. It would soon stop at the whim of the Makers. Then all would be silence.

Except. . . that wasn't how it had to be. I walked over to the flying machine, and slowly, oh so slowly, began to wind its spring.

I climbed inside and strapped myself into the seat. There were three keys in front of me. I turned the first one and heard the hum of turning springs. I would fly this machine, past the Hag, past the crystal stars, past the Copper Mother, past the Twins, and towards the lamp of the Sun. Would I find the Makers waiting for me? Was this what they wanted me to do? I turned the second key, and the machine turned, pointing toward the static sky. I wished so much that Dominique was with me.

This is my third sin. The sin of pride and hubris. I reject my place in this world, to break the barriers of the world and to fly to the Makers, just as Icantari did. I wonder if the wildings will see me fly. I will speak to the Makers and demand that they alter the course of the world. Demand that a thousand years be extended into an infinity.

I turn the final key, and the machine bursts like a flame into the night sky.

About the Author

Deborah Walker grew up in the most English town in the country, but she soon high-tailed it down to London, where she now lives with her partner, Chris, and her two young children. Find Deborah in the British Museum trawling the past for future inspiration or on her blog: http://deborahwalkersbibliography.blogspot.com/

Her stories have appeared in Nature's Futures, Cosmos, Daily Science Fiction, and *The Year's Best SF 18.*

*****~~~~~*****

Heart-Shaped

by Manuel Royal

Hey! You look lost. C'mon in. No, get'cha ass in here. I don't care what your instruction packet says— Kid, look at the name on the door. Right.

Finally! Sit down. Relax, for Christ's sake. Yeah, schedule says you're supposed to go to Orientation. Screw that. I'll orientate you right here and now.

Don't sit on the edge of your chair, Son, sink back in it. Nice, right?

Now, take a look at this thing: your basic fancy heart-shaped candy box. Today is the day, after all, for such things. February 14. Splits the month down the middle. This box came by special courier, addressed to me; yet there's no return address on the package. Is it really innocent nougat and buttercreams? Could be anything. Maybe I should open it up and take a peek, eh?

You want to say no, right? That's what the manual says. You read the manual, of course? It's occasionally useful. I wrote most of it. Caution and procedure get you through the workday, usually, but the rest is a giant crapshoot.

Trust me. Field Commander for the whole Southeast Zone, that's right. Decades of experience, and the scars to prove it. Almost a thousand field men report to guys who report to me. Surely, you must think, I'll make the smart choice regarding this box here, like the ideal commander in the manual. Vigilance! Yes?

Okay, the War. Now, the War between them and us is entering something like its fifty thousandth year. Nobody knows just when it started, right, which is why there's not a holiday and a parade every year. Also because it's the biggest secret in the world.

41

Crack a smile, it's okay. Sure, I take it serious. Never doubt it's a serious thing. It's a War, not a pillow fight, Kid, even if it does involve pillows and fighting. And sometimes pillow fights. So the human race—fwit!— is split right down the middle, always has been. Over three billion per side, and just a select few highly qualified swinging dicks like you and me get recruited into the big Super-Secret Pillow Fight. I mean, the War.

Everybody knows it, even if they don't know they know. They feel it deep down, somewhere, sometime. It's down in the bones, down in the blood. Deeper than that, even. Valentinus himself, Saint so-called Valentine—I'm pretty sure he had Klinefelter Syndrome. Extra X chromosome. That's like having a goddamn fifth columnist in every cell in your body.

Saint Valentine got his head chopped off, but he's still giving headaches to every guy in the Western world. Hell of a lot of greeting cards. And candy.

Lost my thread. Okay, the human race—yeah, put your hand down. I know, sexual dimorphism goes back a billion years. But plants and bugs and prairie dogs ain't advanced enough to get fucked-up in the head about it. So: the human race. Split in two by Mother Nature's genetic axe, and that's a bloody, vertical wound. Each half can never be a whole. There's always blood between the two at the places they touch, but the alternative is drying up untouched and withering to a husk, and ergo there's the War, and hence, us. Vigilance!

Can't keep your eyes off that box, can you? I like pretty things too. Velvet, and lace. Here, smell. Nice, right? But you're thinking it might blow us both to Hell. Me, an alcoholic, used-up old bastard, and you with your fresh face and your certificate, so much potential, assigned to my zone and then zapped your first day. Goddamn heartbreaking. But you and I and every Guardsman out there are living a heartbeat away from getting blown up or

42

burnt down every single day. Or crushed or bisected or something real unpleasant.

Have some Scotch. Save it—we all drink, Son.

Yeah, bisected, I was saying, like what happened to the guy who sat behind this desk before me. Brought it on himself really, cause he was a traitor. In a way, anyway. And not because he slept with the enemy. Hell, we all sleep with the enemy. You do it, I do it. I expect you to do it.

No, what he did was, he tried to make the job easy for himself. Started taking Anteros capsules. Don't pretend you don't know what that is, Kid, I can see you do. Maybe you even tried it? Sure you did. I don't want men without a curiosity streak. I'm a curious bastard myself. Curiouser and curiouser.

The capsules, sure, they work. Full sexual function, without any messy tender feelings. You can sail through enemy waters and never lose your compass. No attachment. Deep cover assignments, hit-and-run, what have you; swallow the caps, and you're an emotionally bulletproof rutting machine. No baggage, no distractions, no gasps and sighs, and no sleepless nights mooning over her. Vet it, hit it, quit it, use what you've learned to plant the thingamajig, copy the documents, blow up the whatsit, take out the enemy strategic waypoint or neutralize their asset, what have you.

In other words, you'll be just like—I mean, emotionally, aside from your set of super-secret skills— just like a certain percentage of the male population already is by nature. Those guys are what we call assholes. You ever wonder why we don't recruit those assholes?

Because a man with no feelings about the enemy has got no stake in the war. A man who can't be cut is a man with no edge. No, strike that, that's stupid. I meant to say, a man who never wants something more than he wants life itself won't have the keen anticipation of loss that he needs, to, ah, to keep from getting himself bisected by a goddamn Handmaiden.

By the way, they're not fembots, or succubots, or automotarts, or gynoid killstrike units or any other name you might hear. The female geniuses who created them called them Handmaidens, and you've got to respect their centuries of work. That's right, Jack, centuries, perfecting lethal robot women. When you reach clearance level to read Ben Franklin's 1779 assessment of Claire Rameau's work, you'll see what I mean. Thank God for the Reign of Terror, right? Never mind, you'll see.

Handmaidens. Those things are amazing, and if it weren't for our bioengineered pythons, and, of course, focused induction cannons, we'd have very little to counter them.

Know your enemy, respect your enemy, destroy your enemy.

Anyway—this guy I was droning on about popped those Anteros capsules like breath mints, and they dropped his EQ—that's a real thing, Emotional Quotient, down to nothing. Work on your EQ, boy, it can be the best tool on your belt.

So, he lost his edge—I say edge, but you can call it tenderness. Yeah. Tenderness requires emotional awareness—EQ—and sensitivity, of which he had none, so he missed the little nuances that might've told him he was about to reach a parting of ways with himself. Handmaiden cut him in half, right down the middle. Obviously she still had her edge. If it were up to me, we'd put that guy in a museum, or maybe two museums, as a cautionary exhibit.

Back to this pretty red heart-shaped box with velvet and lace on the outside, and the nice card. Could be—maybe Semtex or something? Yes? No, you're missing the point. No, it's not anthrax, you're missing— no, it's not nanobots, there are no fucking nanobots.

44

Nanobots are always ten years away. Jesus, Kid. You're missing the point.

Read the card while I untie the ribbons.

You know it's never going to end, right? Long as we're talking frankly here? There ain't no permanent victory on the horizon, or down the pike. That's why our watchword is Vigilance!, not Victory! Look, there've been three honest-to-god matriarchies in history—not written history, maybe, but in reality—and no telling how many patriarchies, and then whatever the hell we've got going these days. Doesn't matter, it always comes back to some kind of balance.

Okay, true, in about twenty years they're gonna have parthenogenesis down, and it'll be fucking Judgment Day around here. Have fun with that; I'll be dead by then. But we got guys working on countermeasures already.

Okay, history: you think it mattered when they got the vote a hundred years ago? No, it didn't. Politics, ordinary wars, religions—all that stuff's on the surface. Nothing in the public arena ever addresses our War without hiding under some level of disguise. Listen to the radio late at night; sometimes a country & western song or a soul tune'll just about get it right. Old stuff, I mean, not that crap they're makin' now. George Jones. Ray Charles. Leonard Cohen. It's all there. Man, I don't know how we didn't recruit him.

Fanny Brice did a torch song in 1923 that literally described an ongoing Brooklyn-based operation. You don't know who that is. No, she wasn't an active; had no clue. Just one of those things. Yeah, it is funny. Turned into a thing, and we lost six men keeping that record off the streets. Six guys just like you, stone dead and bloody under the Fifth Avenue Elevated.

Vigilance! It's always been our memorably unimaginative motto. You know what their motto is? It's three words. Eat, Pray, Love. Heh, just kidding. No, it's: Fight Every Day.

Okay, ribbons done, let's lift the lid on this baby. You ready? I'll do it fast. Whee!

Take it easy, Kid. Here, have one. Yummy, yummy chocolates. See, I'm eating one. Mm-mm. Strawberry cream.

You get it, right? No, forget the manual, just think. Taking me out with a rigged package would be child's play. These are grown women, they know what they're doing. This isn't a bomb, it's just a lovely heart-shaped box of chocolates, given by a woman to a man rather than vice versa. Yeah, let that sink in.

It's happening all over the country, thanks to a nationwide campaign of whispers and hints and barely discernable nudges, a program so subtle that calling it "propaganda" or even "behavioral modification" is an insult. Me, I just would've done a big splashy ad campaign. But, no: way too obvious for them. Multiply this nice box by about fifty million. Sure, they call it a fad, but any good Guardsman knows it's another encroachment on our front, and it ain't going away. They never give up a toehold. Here on out, they own this holiday.

So you see, right, the momentary advantage of vaporizing me would be insignificant compared to the destructive force from this reversal of the box-of-candy dynamic. Have another chocolate, and gimme that card.

Let's see. Poem. Listen:

My Luminary.
Summer lightning, cherry heat, burning sparks.
Illuminate me, my amber glowing sunset, my
cannon's yellow flash and flaming ruin, my
torches high, my firebrand, my
crackling hot hearth of home.
You reveal me, shine through my soft flesh, white
heat, you fill me, flare up, flame out, vanish, gone.

That's bad, right? I'm no Lit major, but that sounds like some bad poetry. Doesn't matter. I love her for it. That's right, I love her, and I hate her. If you can't do both, you're no Guardsman.

They really do fight every day. Every day, every hour. They fight with all their hearts.

That's why I won't tolerate any man doping with Anteros in my Zone. A man on that stuff has half a heart at best.

Hey, these toffee ones are great. Try dipping it in your Scotch. Good, right? Don't waste a drop, Son, that booze is older than you are.

Oh, my God—this one's got bacon in it, right inside the chocolate. Very subtle, but I can—that's how they get you.

Listen, I was saying, you can learn every trick, know all the lore, you can be sharp and, yeah, vigilant, and be a really good Guardsman. But only if you fall in love and break your heart, and moan and hurt and go through all that shit, can you ever be a great Guardsman and get a medal. Probably posthumous.

Then the next time you fall for one of them—the second time, I mean, nobody's ready the first time—the next time, you'll turn those rose-colored glasses into night-vision goggles and see the enemy with pitiless clarity. You'll forge that sweet hot pain in your chest into a rose-red laser beam and char the enemy hollow.

You'll take every golden goddamn drop of love inside you, and turn that love into fuel, Son, and hammer your heart into a heart-shaped steel-clad engine of destruction, and you'll roar out there, infiltrate, overwhelm, and obliterate the enemy.

Or make up your own metaphor. Fuck it, I'm drunk. Not a poetry guy. Maybe that Luminary poem isn't so bad. She does enjoy burning things, like for instance my house and our Baton Rouge substation; guess that's why all the fire imagery.

Might as well keep the card in the file. Look here. No, just above the sealed-with-a-kiss lip print—and by the way, that's as good as a fingerprint, I'd know those lips a mile away. I wrote the Cheiloscopy chapter in the manual, but it needs updating. Anyway, look at the initials. Know who that is?

Sure you do, Lad; use your head. That's right. I'm a Field Commander, she's a Battlemistress. They definitely have cooler titles than we do. Her office is down in Mobile instead of here in Atlanta. I keep tabs. She swims naked in the Gulf at night, can you believe that? Strong legs. Long and strong.

She and I, we've been—I mean, after I broke her cover and she moved out of the house—we've been in the same room exactly twice. First time cost me a skull fracture, not to mention two Guardsmen out on long-term disability. Second time, I lost—and this is some delightful Biblical irony, I guess—lost a rib. Right here. I thought she was dead that time, but she sent me a card in the hospital. It said, "Third time's the charm, Darling!"

I can just see her eyes crinkling up in a smile when she wrote that. She's got one of those smiles—well, I presume you've seen the Active Menace list, so you know what that smile looks like. Those cheekbones—anyway.

There have been losses. Personal and otherwise. Personal doesn't really matter in the long run. Except it does. Hell, I lost the best years of my life, f'r Christ's sake, because of her amazing—because of her lies, and now she's got the balls to send me chocolates filled with her sweet love-poison. Metaphorically, I mean. Seriously, it's just chocolate, eat it. Leave the toffees, they're mine.

So, yeah, getting a box of chocolates from my goddamn ex-wife is harder to deal with than some stupid bomb. Jesus, I miss her. We talk, though, almost every week. Third time's coming, that third meeting, she's been hinting all around it. I suspect we'll end up skulking through the Alabama woods, naked, knives in our teeth, stalking each other until it's over. That one's not even a metaphor.

Forget it, Kid, it's the War, it's just the goddamn War. Remember your training, keep your ears and eyes open, you'll do okay.

And remember: Fight every day. I mean, Vigilance!

About the Author

Manuel Royal was born, like Tristram Shandy, with a broken nose. He will die. In between, he lives and writes in Atlanta, Georgia.

*****~~~~~*****

Abbreviated Epics

A Wolf Is Made

by Jordan Ashley Moore

It was daybreak when we set out, and there were some who came to see us, or they were there making their own way and only looked at us. I took Bredhi, because he was capable and he knew the way, and he was a good hunter himself. He liked me more than he did his master, and that was important to me.

A young boy asked his mother about us, I think. He asked her what a son of Odin is. I didn't see them, I was thinking about the deer that would come down to the fields, and the cold water. She didn't say it loudly, but she said what they all say, that it means death and madness, to belong to that god. Because of the way I came here and what I've done for myself they know me. They know what I am. They believe it, or they don't, but they know it.

It was cold that day, and it never warmed up. We heard the first movements in the distance when we walked the horses outside the forest, and into it, but they were too far away. Bredhi led us, patiently, taking in the imprint of their feet, threading his way carefully around the crisp branches and pine needles. He was capable, good with everything he did, because he had to be. I respected that. He didn't have the sheep or cattle or the roof his master did, but he was equal in every other way, and maybe more. I let him choose the path.

When we were far enough along in the morning and the sun had just started to pass over us, I stopped him.

"I'd like to hunt alone," I said. "You go on, get what you can. We'll meet back here." There was a bank of snow, between the trees, almost like a little hill. He smiled a little, nodding to himself, and went off, keeping his eyes on the ground.

I took my time and went north, where the hills started, and set a place. They come there in the morning where they can be hidden, working toward the low places where they can find water. I took the first buck just when he looked at me, as if he knew. At that distance I can hit a mark, like with Skadhi, the times he would goad me. I would hit nine to his seven, most times, but it was the other times that bothered me. They die quickly when the wound is like that, in the throat, and I chased it down easily, finding it lying in the red snow after leaving my horse for a little.

Then the wind came up, and there was a long time of it. I went north, after a while, after noon, under the clouds, feeling somehow wasteful, or incomplete. I was thinking about a woman of the town, how in all my years there I had never taken a wife. I could hold Ingibjorg with her light hair and make love to her. But she was always so far away from me in the ways that mattered. I know people were talking about that. But it wasn't time. It felt like that day. I was following it, but there wasn't enough time, it wasn't right.

I saw the buck, a tall one with fine horns and strange colors. He was aware of me; he skirted out of my sight, leading me into the valley, very deep in the mists. I was agitated, and impatient; I kept thinking about Skadhi, and his servant, who was making his way surely and slowly where I couldn't see him. I drew around the deer a number of times. It seemed human, almost, after a while, the way it led me. But finally I herded it, and let it come to a river. The shot wasn't good, and it would be a slow death, it felt wrong coming out. And I knew it, I knew something was wrong with this day.

I found its blood in the snow and along the banks, in the valleys. But I never found the body. I was furious, and powerless. I knew what was out there and couldn't come to it. Gradually it left the low places and came back to the forest, into the thicker parts, where I couldn't follow with my horse. Late in the day, when it was already dark because of the clouds, I had to decide to leave it, because there would be cutting and cleaning, and it would be too late. I had to leave my work where no one would find it, or see it.

I still walked slowly, and quietly, but I couldn't keep my mind in it, I was so angry. The tall, sparse trees passed by, and I didn't look at them. I had conceded. That was a mistake; on the other side of the valley, where the woods were thickest, I heard a noise to my side, and froze. The brown sullen eyes looked at me, and I couldn't move. I hadn't recognized the snort, but I knew now. The boar stood looking at me sidelong, with its skin glistening a little in the late light, looking almost gold with the clouds on it. It was as long as my horse, with thick, rutted skin. I felt it move forward, a little, deciding. I remembered the men I had seen taken by boars and what they looked like when they were found. I had my knife, but my spear was across my back. And again, wrongly, somehow, the boar put its head down and crept away, disappearing in the brush. It felt strange, like it shouldn't have happened. The boar is Frey's animal, and I wondered what it saw in me to turn its face.

Bredhi was at the earlier site, by the drift, drinking water calmly with his things set out, all three of the deer set out carefully, but not proudly.

"Are you alright, sir?" he asked me. "There was a boar around, earlier."

"Yes," I said. I looked at the three carcasses, very clean ones, beautiful. "Very good work," I admitted.

"Thank you," he said. He didn't look at the body over my shoulder. "There's been a lot of mist. It hasn't been a good day for it." He said it honestly.

"No," I agreed.

I set the body down in the snow and started to clean it, with my back to him, not looking at him. He was so quiet, so modest, so content to do what he was asked.

The buck had led me through the day, and let me shoot it, and turned into nothing. I thought about the walk home, how he would carry his three and my one. My face was warm as I thought about those same men and women who had seen us this morning, how they had been curious. They wanted to know what would happen.

This man didn't have to worry about these things. He didn't have power over himself, he only had to do what he was asked. It didn't matter to him, and there was something wrong with that. I couldn't leave that buck alone, the one I knew was out there. Those kills don't matter. No one would ever see it. No one would know.

I sat him down, to eat what we had brought from home, and looked at him.

"I admire you," I said. "You know what you're about. You do good work."

"Thank you, sir," he said. "I just do what I can."

And he meant it. He was only performing a task.

"We're both from outside," I went on. "We're not from around here. You understand that, right? People think differently about us."

"I do," he said. "That's why I've always taken to you."

I didn't even answer him. I looked in the dead eyes and felt the blood on my hand. A slave had overtaken me, in my own land. I turned and put the knife in his throat, working it like I had with the wounded buck. He didn't ask me anything, he didn't speak. He just tried to fight me off, with his aging, tough hands. He was small, but strong. I looked at him in the snow, and I buried him in the huge snow drift, looking for all the blood that was left, even of the deer. I covered all of it, and felt the blood in my ears. Then I went home, I forced myself to, although it seemed wrong, again, like there was something there I couldn't face.

I carried the three carcasses, though I didn't want to. When I came home in the evening Skadhi was waiting

54

for me, looking out into the dark for his slave, his trusted slave.

"Where is he?" he asked me.

"He rode off into the forest," I said. "I don't know where he went."

He didn't say anything, he just looked out a moment more and then went off, behind me. I should have said more, but I couldn't. I couldn't try any harder to hide it.

I had already washed my hands, in the river, but I uncovered them and washed them again. I lay down in my hall and tried to sleep, and heard the first stirrings of doubt outside, but couldn't find the will to fight it, or get away.

Before the sun rose Ingibjorg came to my door and told me what they had done.

"They found Bredhi," she said. She wouldn't look at me. "You'd better go."

I tried to explain myself, or keep her there, but I couldn't. I could hear Skadhi shouting outside, talking loudly enough for me to hear, saying they had found him in the huge bank, and the way his body was bruised and frozen, in the ice. He told them what sort of man I was. They would call that place Bredhadrift, he said. He didn't come and say it to me. I left before they could come. I rode out quietly in the morning and moved north, and west, in the same forest but the remoter part of it. I knew I had to leave it all, and it wasn't just my home, or that region. They would be saying my name in the temples now. They would be saying I was a wolf, a murderer, and no one could escape that. But it would take time, they would have to outlaw me. I couldn't come to my father, but I turned my way toward him, in the forests, in the hidden places. I had my things with me, what I could carry, and I would have to survive.

I know how to live. I lived in the cold nine nights. On that ninth I saw a shadow moving in the firelight, and a raven cawed. I thought I knew him, but I was afraid, because I was hunted.

"Who's there?" I said. Nothing answered, and I only felt the terror of taking Bredhi's life, suddenly, everything I had done, and the way the blood had made me feel. I sat in silence and saw the shadow of an old man, not looking at me, turned to the trees, or the moon.

"You get to be the wolf, now," he said. I sat and shivered, and tried to understand. And because of the blood on the snow and my heart I wondered if this could be real, the world I entered after taking Bredhi's life. I looked at the man who made us, and has us unmake each other. He was only clear to me then, when I could still feel the warmth on my face and the blood on my hands. This is what he almost said to me, standing silent in the dark, that he is only clear when we are animals, and tear at each other. The man who turns us into wolves.

I was a wolf, because of what I'd done. I would hide, and be turned away, and feed on wounds. I was called a thief by my people and my god; and it was my truth, my reason. I looked at the figure in the dark, living in the mist. They didn't believe.

They think I live in the mists and lie to myself. But my god and my father are with me, I make him, and he makes me, I become close to him. Only he can understand, and make use of me. I know this world is made with death and the things between death and our lives. I know what stands in the mist, and how close I am to it.

I hear the wolves and the birds in the west, by the sea. I have to follow them, because they are his, he made them with his hands, and there is nothing else, because I am one of them.

###

About the Author

Jordan Ashley Moore lives in Walker, Louisiana, with his two crazy cats and a loyal Miniature Dachshund. His short stories have appeared in Necrotic Tissue and also in *Origins: Colliding Causalities,* from Third Flatiron.

*****~~~~~*****

Abbreviated Epics

Through An Ocular, Darkly

by Martin Clark

While sailing to Byzantium, we floundered

I found myself breathing in time to the slow beat of a heavy-bladed ventilation fan. The blinds drawn against the glare of a Constantinople summer imbued my workshop with a sepia hue, as if it were a photographic composition. Gordon Pasha's bribe lay heavily in my pocket, a constant reminder of prostituted loyalty.

Josephus the Tailor glared at me over his half-moon spectacles. "You, Leon Prinz, you were commissioned to build an automaton, a neo-golem to defend the Temple. Not this, this *toy*."

In reply I caressed my life-sized ballerina on the nape of her neck, activating the flash-steam boiler. She pirouetted and executed a flawless *grand battement*, striking my erstwhile patron in the face before he could react or cry out. The Pharisee fell in an untidy heap, dead before reaching the bare floorboards. She lapsed into second position, her murderous sequence complete.

There was very little blood.

I feared no retribution, as Josephus had been acting alone in an attempt to further his standing amongst the Jewish community. However, I had been bribed by an agent of the Occupation Authority to remove him from the body politic, as casually as one might pluck a chess piece from the board. Accordingly, I devoted his payment towards one of my own projects—the ballerina—in a case of the end becoming the means.

I raised my voice. "Ras!"

The youth appeared from beyond the beaded curtain almost instantly. He was of Romany stock; I had encountered him while travelling through Banat and

59

secured his release from the local magistrate. His slim body, dark curls, and knowing eyes distracted many clients—both male and female—during negotiations over the price for my wares.

The body on the floor drew no glance from him. "Master?"

"Go to the café in Haga Square and ask for Mehmed. Tell him you work for me and that I have a carpet to be moved. He will understand."

Ras gave me a sly smile. "I am well known as your boy, master, and need no introduction. If he raises the matter of payment, what should I say?"

I shook my head. "He owes me a favour. I may not be here when you return, so make sure everything is in order before you abscond for the afternoon."

He bowed, "Master," and left in a rattle of beads.

I had a carefully fostered reputation as a pederast, which opened some doors and closed others. The important thing as a *yabanci*, a foreigner, was to let the locals believe they knew me. Most Europeans made the mistake of remaining aloof, whereas day-to-day life in the great city was nothing if not intimate.

Now alone I turned to the Jung-phone and set the copper headset against my temples. Immediately I was assailed by phantoms; snatches of conversation, random thoughts, the detritus of dreams. Navigating the collective unconscious was more art than science, and a weak mind was easily distracted. I concentrated and was rewarded by the sound of a bell, rung by telekinesis.

A female voice answered, in English but with a French accent. *"Galata. The Office of General Gordon."* The Occupation Authority was housed in that part of the city overlooking the Golden Horn. From this vantage above the harbour they controlled the former Ottoman ministries, and a wise man did not offend them.

"This is Leon Prinz, in Jeter Lane. Please inform Gordon Pasha that his commission is complete."

Through an Ocular, Darkly

"One moment." There was a pause, the suggestion of a muffled conversation outwith my hearing. *"There is something we wish you to inspect. It will be delivered within the hour."*

The *click* of a terminated call brought no finality to my situation, as I had hoped. The promise, the assurance, of a single act of betrayal on my part seemed to be fading like smoke on the breeze. I removed the phone and set it aside before pouring myself a small glass of sherry as a restorative.

The Sultan had appointed General Gordon, the hero of Khartoum, as governor of Istanbul to pacify this most fractious of cities. Instead his rule, and particularly the corps of Christian "Special Constables," had stoked the fires of dissent into an inferno of revolt. Such had been the violence directed against foreigners that the various European military legations had acted in rare consort to impose order on the metropolis. The Sultan had fled to Ankara, leading to a collapse of the Ottoman administration and sparking a general uprising throughout the troubled Balkans.

Now the metropolis was once again "Constantinople," with the grasping Greeks clamouring for its return. Of course the Russians also sought control of the Dardanelles, a move opposed by the English to safeguard their Mediterranean lines of communication. Behind the façade of Occupation Authority cooperation, the "Great Game" continued unabated. These were dangerous times for one such as I, a Christian renegade formally employed by the Ottoman Ministry of Culture.

I retired to my study to wait upon events.

…

It transpired that "within the hour" constituted almost two, but in their defence the tarpaulin-covered pallet carried by eight perspiring Royal Marines looked disagreeably heavy. The armed detail was accompanied by McBride, the representative of Gordon Pasha and the

61

closest most civilians came to the great man himself. McBride was a burly Scot of uncertain temper and not someone I wished to antagonise. The Marines deposited their burden in my workshop and took up sentry positions.

McBride helped himself to my whisky and joined me in contemplating the strange device that now lay uncovered before us. In shape it roughly resembled an artillery shell, some eight feet in length and three in diameter, with articulated fins at one end—folded in two—and radial pistons at the other. An outer skin of panels had been removed, exposing a bewildering complexity of pipes, gears, and electrical wiring. Beneath my fingers, I detected a slight vibration.

My guest gestured with his glass. "The damndest thing, eh? We recovered it from the wreckage of that dirigible stolen by the anarchists. Cornelius, their self-styled 'Captain-General' offered to sell us its secrets." He snorted. "As if we have anything to learn from a Prussian gas-bag. Fortunately, the thieves turned out to be both politically naive *and* aeronautically inept, which saved us the time and effort of shooting them down."

I frowned. "So this is the property of the Kaiser? The German legation will not take kindly to any unauthorised examination."

"No, it's not theirs, not by a long chalk. In fact none of the other Great Powers lay claim to it, not even the Americans. You'd almost think they know something we don't."

"And so you bring it to me?"

McBride shrugged and finished his drink. "Well, the navy engineers had a look-see, but this level of automation is beyond even the most intricate self-correcting gun sight currently in service. It will take our experts several days to reach here from England, and we may not have the luxury of waiting that long."

My suspicions were instantly aroused. "Your meaning?"

He set down the glass and pointed towards the nose. "You observe those six pistons? One has been dropping each day since the device was recovered. Now only two remain."

I took a step back. "And the need for caution somehow escapes you? Send this, this *contraption* to sea and have it pitched overboard."

The fool laughed. "And here was I thinking you were a slave to curiosity, Prinz. '

"Curiosity does not benefit the dead, sir."

"Inspect the other side of our enigma and tell me if you still feel the same."

I did as he suggested, but what I discovered simply added confusion to my growing sense of unease: rows of dials similar to those found on a combination lock.

McBride joined me. "The top row shows the date in the form of eight digits, the next three are times expressed in hours, minutes, and seconds, and the last, I have it on good authority, represents a barometric altimeter. Initially we believed this to be some kind of complex timing mechanism, but it transpires the third and fourth rows actually represent latitude and longitude. Strangely, all the settings correspond to the time and place of the Great Exhibition back in 'fifty-one, which is obviously a meaningless coincidence. The dial array is locked in position and can't be freed without a six-bladed key. We summoned the best cracksmen in Constantinople, only to be told the lock cannot be picked and duplicating the key will take weeks. Damned inconvenient."

I ran a finger along each row of dials. "No, this cannot constitute a detonator. But why would the operation of this device require orientation in three dimensions?"

McBride shrugged. "You have twenty hours in which to inspect this oddity and uncover its secrets. Thereafter it will, as you predicted, be jettisoned at sea.

The torpedo-ram Thunder Child is being prepared for immediate departure should the need arise."

I stood for a moment; hand on chin, gazing at my new commission. "And if I should prove unequal to the task?"

He grunted. "I will return tomorrow to discover what you have learned. You would be wise not to disappoint us, Herr Prinz."

I bowed as he took his leave, ever the obedient servant. Six of the Marines departed with him, leaving two on guard, or perhaps as my gaolers. I rubbed my eyes. "Ras! Tea! And bring more each hour."

A surly murmur was my only reply, as he had been disappointed to return in the company of Mehmed only to find me still in residence. The device now stood upon the spot where Josephus had fallen, thankfully obscuring the sand-covered blood stain. I removed my jacket and hung it carefully upon a hanger, then began my inspection.

It soon became apparent I was dealing with an approximation of design, not its true expression. In the manner of a competent watchmaker duplicating a Faberge masterpiece, his creation may aspire to the same function, but at the expense of elegance and simplicity. If thought is father to the deed then this offspring must have proved somewhat of a disappointment.

I moved on, and soon determined the folded stabilization fins were actually cooling vanes. Opening them into their full position produced an immediate increase in surface temperature—which raised the question of what internal mechanism was generating this heat in the first place. After a moment's thought I smiled to myself. The pistons were providing daily fuel to a flash-steam boiler, merely a larger version of those used to power my own creations. I had observed such a closed design aboard a diving bell, with the combustion exhaust gases being lodged in a tank for later venting.

Through an Ocular, Darkly

Pleased at my progress, I switched attention to the inspection port; a short kaleidoscope which revealed only a darkened interior. It was the screw thread around the lip which provided inspiration, recalling the eyepiece on my Zeiss "Serpent."

This articulated tube facilitated internal inspection of automata without the need for time-consuming disassembly. Hurriedly, I detached the magnifying array from my own equipment and gently screwed it into place. Imagine my disappointment when the interior image remained stubbornly blank. However, there was a slight play in the assembly which suggested a spring-loaded switch, so I pressed home and was rewarded by an audible *click*.

A beam of lurid blue light sprang from the lens to strike the wall opposite.

I fell back, aghast, choking off a cry of terror. I had witnessed such illumination only once before, during my time at the Académie de Fabrication in Landes. The Académie de Fabrication, now reduced to a poisonous crater shunned by the local inhabitants. At the heart of the device before me lay no conventional power source, but the barely constrained fury of a Rutherford-Curie generator.

"Master?" Ras stood in the doorway bearing my tea upon a silver tray. He stared at the light from Hell. "Should I start packing?"

I took a moment to compose myself, rather than display moral weakness in front of a menial. "There is danger here, yes, but I am in full command of the situation. Now, leave the tea and go about your business. I am not to be disturbed."

He set down the glass, bowed, and withdrew. The hot, sweet liquid was welcome, but I spilled more than I consumed, my hand quivered so. Rutherford-Curie generators were notoriously fickle, requiring near-constant adjustment by a team of expert technicians. Failure to adequately regulate the radium surges could prove catastrophic, as the world had learned to its cost. The complexity of an automated system which could accomplish such a task filled me with awe and dread in equal measure. Repairing to my study I took a pinch or two of cocaine, and, thus fortified, returned to the mental fray.

Time passed, unheeded. Ras brought more tea and slivers of melon to sustain my efforts. I worked on, cautiously freeing some of the smaller sub-assemblies from the central frame for scrutiny – but not detaching any tubes or wiring – before setting them back in place. The fog of confusion began to lift.

The device was entirely self-contained, of that I was certain. There were no inlet or outlet valves which would allow the circulation of water and steam between the generator and an external source. Furthermore, by pressing my ear against various parts of the exterior I was able to locate the distinctive "crinkle" of a condensation chamber. Self-contained, but to what end? There had been talk of using the so-called "Radium Engine" as a weapon, but I refused to accept that such obvious ingenuity had been deployed merely in the service of wanton destruction.

I provided myself with a further, more generous, measure of cocaine in search of mental insight. Restless, I paced to-and-fro in my study, attempting to fathom the thought process behind the creation of such an enigmatic device.

A six-bladed key.

I cursed at my own stupidity. This was a "Landes key," designed by the great Georges Bouton prior to his untimely demise. The cut of each blade was a masterpiece of intricacy—but not unique between locks, as it was the orientation which was critical. The unwary had only a one-in-six chance of inserting a Landes key correctly, and turning it against orientation would irreparably jam the locking mechanism.

I had such a key in my bureau, a memento of sorts from the *Académie.*

It lay heavy in my hand as I stood before the infernal machine, contemplating my fate. The obvious solution would be to surrender the key to McBride and let him hazard all at his discretion. Yet my curiosity and professional pride would not have it so. I was locked in an abstract battle of wits with the designer, the great intelligence, who had seemingly tamed the Radium Engine and bent it to his will. Some part of me, no doubt bouyed by pharmaceutical courage, resolved to match his achievements and make them my own.

The key slid home, smoothly.

I closed my eyes.

It turned.

The machine chattered. I blinked, my earlier confidence now replaced by consternation as both remaining pistons slid home. The dials rotated as if subject to some unseen hand, while I looked on, fascinated. With a final flare the lurid blue light winked out, leaving a discernable scorch mark on the plaster. I laughed in triumph. Now, whatever the true function of the device, I was its master.

And yet my satisfaction was tempered by confusion. Instead of each dial returning to zero, as I had anticipated when they first began to move, the device now displayed a new set of seemingly arbitrary coordinates. Certainly the "date" was nonsense—it lay over two hundred years in the future—and the altitude indicated was in the region of thirty-three *thousand* feet above sea level. I began to fear that this incoherence was due more to damage than design, with potentially dire consequences for the continued safe regulation of the Rutherford-Curie generator.

I walked around to the inspection port, my attention drawn by an audible ticking of which I had previously been unaware. The eyepiece assembly was rotating at the rate of approximately one degree per second, to no discernable purpose, and the interior view was once again dark. More mystified than concerned, I turned away to inspect the damaged plaster. As I feared, the affected area was giving off sufficient heat so as to prevent me placing my palm flat upon the blistered surface. I resolved to have the entire wall rebuilt and the debris dumped in the Lesser Harbour.

Behind me the clicking ceased, only to be replaced by a raw, irregular, whine. The rising note built rapidly towards a crescendo. It was the sound I associated with the imminent electrical discharge of a Tesla coil, and the sound of my doom. I spun around to find the eyepiece glowing with the white-hot fire of oblivion—and was consumed.

...

"Action stations, action stations. All hands, prepare to break for high orbit. This is not a drill. I repeat, this is not a drill." The voice was male, distorted as by a megaphone.

I lay sprawled on a metal grating, while icy water sprayed my fevered skin. My pain had no voice; it was beyond expression. I struggled to breathe, I struggled to stay sane. The spray ceased, leaving me feeling as if exposed to a combination of hoarfrost and furnace. Unseen hands placed a thick blanket around my shoulders. I raised my head.

A young woman stood before me, hand on hip. She was dark-haired, severe of feature, wearing an unfamiliar uniform jacket and straight skirt – the hem of which ended fully eighteen inches above her ankles. At least modesty prevailed in the shape of long leather boots. She spoke in English but with a Russian accent.

"Welcome to the future, Herr Prinz. It has been waiting for you."

About the Author

Martin Clark is a freelance writer and occasional poet.

He is the author of supernatural noir novellas formally produced by Eggplant Literary Productions (now sadly defunct) now taken on by Tickety Boo Press, and short stories in recent Third Flatiron anthologies. He also contributes to several online publications including Mythaxis.co.uk, Timelesstales.com, and Kraxon.com. His range of subject matter includes science fiction, urban fantasy, romance, and westerns. He puts this down to the somewhat eclectic mobile lending library where he grew up.

He works as a local government officer in south-west Scotland but still finds time to be an evil stepfather.

We'll be looking forward to more stories set in the universe of Dr. Leon Prinz.

*****~~~~~*****

Abbreviated Epics

Damfino Plays for Table Stakes

by Ben Solomon

"You're cleaning up, you are." Spoken by Mr. K. Also known to the boys as "Albert K." or "the brother-in-law." Referred to in public as "Mr. James Clark."

In his private mirror, Albert K. sizes up to be a gambler, raconteur, bon vivant, a man not to be trifled with. The boys fear him as a top enforcer, an organizational hammer, a potential loose cannon. The district attorney's office lists Mr. K. on its "toilet roll," a piece of filth in need of flushing. The three leading dailies, *The Trib, Times,* and *American,* describe him as one of the leading social pestilences of 1929.

"You gutted Peter and Frank there," Mr. K. said. "Adam, too. And Schwimmy." He unscrewed the chewed, soaked cigar stub from his lips and spat on the cement floor. "This tastes like wet lint." He squashed the butt in the ashtray. "What's the name again? Dam what?"

"DAM-FEE-NO."

"That's it. Damfino. Huh. Never heard of you. But Schwimmy says you're okay. Thanks for nothing, Schwimmy. Bet he'd like to take back that introduction, isn't that right, Schwimmy?"

"Happy Valentine's Day to you, too," Schwimmer thought, but never spoke. He and the rest of the boys stationed themselves at the opposite end of the garage. They put all the distance they could between them and the volatile Mr. K.

"So, Mr. Damfino," Mr. K. said, "how do you account for being so damn lucky?"

"I don't."

"Oh, you don't." Mr. K. took out a robusto, unwrapped it. He pinched it, sniffed it, bit the end, and spat. He jammed the cigar between his teeth.

Damfino said, "A gambler who relies on luck is the same as a bootlegger relying on luck."

"Oh, is that right?"

"No different than a soiled shirt."

"Taken to the cleaners, you mean."

"That's what I mean."

"I like that. That's good. So tell me, Mr. Damfino, are you claiming to make your own luck?"

"Providence doesn't belong at the gaming table."

"You're telling me you're that good?"

"Every roll is different."

"So?"

"Today is Thursday, tomorrow is Friday. Today will never be repeated. This day you're born, that day you die."

"You talk funny. Anyone ever tell you that?"

Damfino yawned.

"Well, I don't like it." Mr. K. eyed the stacks of currency in front of Damfino. Both men had drawn their final card. "It comes to this."

Damfino yawned for a second time. "I believe it's my bet."

"Jeez, I'm sorry if I'm boring you, Damfino."

"Table stakes, Mr. K?"

"Yeah. That's right."

"You appear to be tapped out."

Mr. K. ignored the observation by lighting his cigar.

"I'm becoming disinterested," Damfino said. "You must have something worth betting."

Mr. K.'s eyes roved across the garage. Cluttered barrels and crates. Racks of tools. Shelves of used parts. Behind him, at the far end, John May tinkered on a two-tone Caddie. Mr. K. gave Damfino the once-over. He jerked his head towards the auto. "What do you think?"

"Offering up Mr. May?"

"What? No, the car. I'm talking about the Caddie."

72

Damfino fought back another yawn. "I don't need cars. But Mr. May's life—that's intriguing."

Mr. K. leaned forward. "Are you kidding me? You want me to bet his life?"

"Against one hundred dollars."

A look of astonishment screwed up Mr. K.'s pan. It melted quick. He burst out in laughter loud enough to distract everyone in the room.

"That kills me. It really does."

"I'm talking about killing Mr. May," Damfino said.

"Sure you are, sure you are. Okay. I'll bite. I'll see your one hundred against Mr. May's life. That's all he's good for—just a piecemeal mechanic. What have you got?"

Damfino's three of a kind beat two pair. Mr. K.'s fist thumped the table. Peter and Frank peered over a shared newspaper. Heyer and Schwimmer looked up from their ledgers. Weinshank stopped flipping his coin. Mr. May dropped a lug wrench on his hand and popped his thumb in his mouth.

"Give me them cards," Mr. K. said. "We're going to draw, high-low. It's my shuffle."

"You want to get even," Damfino said. "The eternal struggle. If only you hadn't lost all your money."

"Look, you—you—" Mr. K.'s neck turned pink above the starched collar. "You want another life? You want to play it that way? There's plenty more."

"Ah, now you arouse me. Say, two-fifty for Mr. Schwimmer?"

"Schwimmy?" Mr. K. raised his voice. "Jeez, you could have him for another hundred."

"No, let's make it two hundred and fifty dollars."

"It's your funeral. Cut."

Damfino smiled. He wiped the tips of his fingers on the lapel of his jacket. He reached across the table and cut the deck. He displayed a six of spades, then returned the stack. Mr. K. cut, hesitated, then turned over the five of hearts.

"Two out of three?" Damfino said.

"Are you trying to be cute?"

"No one ever gets cute with you, Mr. K."

"You're damn right. Make it two-fifty for Heyer."

"I accept."

Damfino drew the six of clubs. Mr. K. drew the three of diamonds.

"Dammit! Dammit"

The shout froze the other men as they were. Whenever Mr. K. lost his temper was high time to become invisible.

"Again," Mr. K. said. "What'll you give me for Peter and Frank?"

"I don't wish to take advantage."

"How much, Damfino?"

"If you insist?"

"I insist, dammit!"

"Since you demand it, let's say five hundred apiece."

"That's one thousand, then. One thousand for this one hand."

"Agreed."

The two players locked eyes. Damfino cut: the six of spades. Mr. K: the two of hearts.

"You're running out of lives," Damfino said.

Mr. K. sneered. He swallowed hard. He worked the cigar from one corner of his mouth to the other.

Damfino said, "All or nothing, Mr. K.?" Mr. K.'s left eye narrowed. "All the cash in front of me against your life, Mr. K. And I'll kick in the lives of your little gang, here."

"The hell you say."

"Yes. I do. But be warned—"

"Nobody but nobody warns me. Get that? Not the likes of you."

"I get it, all right."

"Nobody."

Mr. K. scooped the cards up fast and began to shuffle. He glared at the cash across the table. He shuffled for a long time. He slapped down the deck.

"Cut," Mr. K. said.

"My pleasure," Damfino said.

A gentle, civil grin graced Damfino's lips as he halved the stack. He rolled his hand slowly to reveal the ace of spades. Mr. K. almost choked on his own spit. He stabbed the cigar from his lips, laid it with care in the ashtray. He cleared his throat twice. Damfino waited patiently, his hands folded on the table. Mr. K. reached for the deck, performed his cut, and flipped his hand over—he exposed the two of hearts.

"I'm afraid you're all dead," Damfino said.

Mr. K. leaned back from the table. He snatched up the cigar and lit a wooden match. The flame danced wildly.

Damfino said, "I've upset you."

Mr. K. made an ugly face as he puffed on the robusto.

Damfino said, "I should be off."

"You're not going nowhere," Mr. K. said.

"I was afraid you'd take this attitude."

"I haven't got me any attitude," Mr. K. said. "I'm telling you. The money stays."

"I see."

"As far as anyone losing their life, you know who's lost *that* bet."

"I see."

Mr. K. leered like a lush staring at the day's first drink.

"My dear Mr. K.," Damfino said, "We have been sitting for hours. You don't mind if I stand? Perhaps freshen up first?"

Mr. K. shook with laughter. "Mind? I wouldn't mind one teensy bit. The door behind you, to your left. Won't do you any good—a pigeon couldn't fit through the window. Go ahead. Freshen up. By all means. Freshen the hell out of yourself."

Damfino smiled politely, rose and bowed. The echoes of Mr. K.'s laughter faded as he closed the little door behind him.

Oil and grease lined the washroom sink. Damfino rinsed his hands with care. As he bent his face toward the tap, he heard the outside garage door slam shut, followed by incoherent shouts. A muffled conversation ensued as he splashed his face with cool water. He turned over the soiled hand towel, searching for a clean spot on the cloth. He distinctly heard, ". . .against the wall." He perceived the shuffling of feet. Then silence.

Damfino gingerly dabbed his face as the tommy guns erupted. The outburst pounded through the air with explosive resonance, persisting for tens of rounds. When the volleys subsided, Damfino tilted his ear to the door. Two shotgun blasts resounded like dynamite. Several sets of feet scuffled hurriedly. The outside door slammed again. Silence.

Damfino exited the washroom, casually, returned to the table through the haze of smoke. He listened momentarily to one set of labored breathing, broken by an occasional moan.

Damfino collected his winnings and left.

About the Author

Ben Solomon grew up with Picasso, Cagney, and Beethoven. Classical arts training, comic books, and Hollywood's golden age rounded out his education and provided inspiration for a lifetime. He's worked across many disciplines, attempting to capture the heart and soul of music onto canvas, translate oils and celluloid into words.

Solomon's passion for the tough guy world of early gangster and PI flicks led to the creation of "The Hard-Boiled Detective," a short story series starring a nameless gumshoe in a throwback era seeking truth, justice, and sometimes a living. He launched the ongoing series online in February 2013, offering three yarns a month to subscribers. His sleuth has appeared in e-zines across the web, as well as the 2014 anthology, *The Shamus Sampler II.* Another adventure is scheduled to appear in an upcoming anthology published by Fox Spirit Books.

Samples and more information about Solomon's old-school crime series can be found here: http://thehardboileddetective.com/

*****~~~~~*****

The Committee

by Margarita Tenser

In the beginning was the meeting. And Lo, the Great God Mellar spake unto the lesser gods, saying, "All right, all right, let's get started, or we'll be even further behind deadline. I hereby call this meeting of the Creationist Committee to order and whatnot. Who's up first?"

And verily, Anaimas, Lord of Hadrons and Keeper of the Minutes, cleared his throat. The other gods all groaned.

"Shut up, you lot," said Anaimas. "I just want to make sure we're getting off on the right foot. To that end, Mellar, could you please refer to us by our full and proper title of Committee for the Creation of All Things, Past and Present, Yea Unto The Full Length and Breadth of the Universe?"

Mellar sighed. "Can't you just put down in the minutes that I said that?" he said, leaning back in his office chair and rubbing his most holy temples with his thumbs.

"I don't know," Anaimas sniffed. "In my mind things ought to be done correctly, that's all. Otherwise, why bother? Speaking of doing things correctly, the first item on the agenda is evolutionary—"

"Speaking of bothering," interrupted Flegmatica, Goddess of Event Horizons and the elected representative of the Energy Sources Subcommittee. "Have we fully settled the question of whether the universe is going to *have* length and mass? I feel like we just went round in circles on this last time."

"We did," said Mellar, glaring down towards the far end of the boardroom table. "If I recall correctly, I ordered that dealt with by this meeting."

"That's right," said Anaimas, flipping through his folder of past minutes. "It says here that you instructed the principal proponents of each argument, Eloi and Piria, to spend as many infinities as they found necessary together until they could work out a reasonable compromise. To which I registered the objection that it's not an efficient use of infinities, but what do I know."

Everybody turned to look at the two unfortunate squabblers, who sat next to each other with their arms (or other relevant appendages) crossed, looking grouchy and slightly sheepish. They were goddesses of Strange and Charm, respectively, and a number of infinities in each other's company had not improved their relationship.

"Well?" demanded Mellar.

Eloi and Piria exchanged glances, before Eloi rolled her eyes slightly and made a little "go-on-then" gesture, and Piria stood up.

"We have decided," she began, grimacing, "That the important thing is for the universe to appear to have length and mass from the perspective of its inhabitants. If this can be accomplished without forcing issues of scale upon innocent fundamental particles, both of us will consider the point moot."

There was a brief silence among the gods, as each divinity contemplated this solution. Then the silence burst into a cacophony of opinions.

"That is the stupidest thing I've ever heard!" the Godling of Combustion shouted, banging its fist on the table.

"Hang on, hang on," said the Goddess of Causality. "I can think of a number of ways to get that done."

"I'm all for it," said Decatyl, the God/dess of Uncertainty, rubbing their chin thoughtfully with one hand as three of their others began to take measurements and draw preliminary sketches.

"Of course you're all for it," sneered the God of Planes.

"And what's that supposed to mean?" demanded Decatyl.

Amidst the din, the Great God Mellar wearily put his head in his hands. Anaimas pursed his lips and reshuffled the minutes, before pulling out a small gong and tapping it with his pen. It made a noise that was technically louder than the entire universe, since sound hadn't been invented yet.

"Right," said Anaimas into the ringing silence that followed. "The first item on the agenda is actually the allocation of evolutionary zones."

The assembled deities groaned, again, in unison.

"Bloody mucky things," said Combustion.

"Of course you'd think that," said Planes.

"Yeah," said Combustion. "I would, 'cause I bloody well do."

"Don't start," said Mellar. "Flegmatica?"

Flegmatica waved a frond and, verily, caused a slide to be projected onto the wall. "I'm still firmly of the opinion that if we arrange galactic matter in the right pattern it will happen, er, organically, as it were," she said, conjuring a laser pointer from somewhere. "Here are some models my team came up with."

Bello, the God of Fluid Dynamics, raised a hand. "I have a counter-proposal," he said.

"Yes?" Flegmatica said, frostily.

"Well," said Bello, "I just don't see why we can't draw straws for someone to murder so we can transform their body into all the stuff organic life-forms need. We could give it a real retro flare. All this modern stuff, it's really just fripperies, isn't it?"

"Oh, no, no, no," said Mellar. "No. No, no, no, no, no."

81

"Damn right," said Piria. "If we go down that route, we ought to make everything out of an egg. Otherwise, what's the point?"

"This is exactly why we formed this committee in the first place," said Mellar. "I'll hear no more about eggs or murder, all right?"

"What about just stuffing everything we've got into a tiny dot until it explodes?" suggested the Godling of Combustion.

"What about just stuffing everything into a tiny dot until it explodes?" mimicked Planes in mocking tones.

"Again," said Causality. "It could be done. However, I fear there would be some really quite irritating side effects."

"Bah!" shouted Combustion.

"Okay, you know what?" said Mellar. "We'll put that down as a contingency plan. Okay, Anaimas? Write down that if we don't get a decent universal structure in place by the deadline, we'll just compress and explode everything."

"Er. . . " said Anaimas. "Are you quite sure, my lord?"

"Bloody hell, am I the chairman, or what?" Mellar shouted.

"All right, all right, keep your toga on," said Anaimas. "I'm only trying to help. I don't know. . . "

"We just need something to motivate us to do this properly," said Mellar. "Don't worry, we won't end up actually using it."

"Of course not," said Flegmatica. "That would just be silly.

###

About the Author

Margarita Tenser is a Soviet-born Aussie who has fewer cats and more odd socks than she'd really like. She has been previously published in Voiceworks and Strange Horizons.

*****~~~~~*****

Abbreviated Epics

Rain Over Lesser Boso

by Gustavo Bondoni

Mariko swore like a sailor as another drop of scalding wax dropped onto her forearm and immediately looked around to make certain that no one was present. All her dreams would be forfeit if she were deemed unworthy.

We wouldn't want that now, would we?

The work was nearly done. Acid-resistant wax covered the entire surface of her umbrella. It was better workmanship than any of the other girls would ever be capable of, but the sight of the thick cloth and ungainly, drooping dome made her understand just how much had been lost. The brilliantly dyed bamboo-and-paper *wagasa,* so popular before the breaking, survived only in the ink drawings on the Samurai's wall and in Mariko's imagination. She carefully wrapped the umbrella in soft cloth.

The afternoon was sunny, and the younger village girls could be seen chasing one another around the dusty square in a way that would never have been permitted when the island still pretended to follow established protocol. She watched them absently, waiting for the call that was imminent. Doubt suddenly assaulted her. What if the promised summons never came?

Do not fret. It will come.

"Mariko?" The voice was imperious and hesitant at the same time, as if knowing that obedience was owed, yet unsure how to react if it was withheld.

"Yes, Mistress?"

"I have wonderful news." The dour look on the woman's pale features gave lie to her words.

"I am listening."

You already know what she's going to say.

"You have been summoned. The Samurai himself wishes an audience with you."

"That *is* wonderful news, Mistress." Actually, most interviews with the local lord ended in punishment, disgrace, sometimes even in death. But it was obvious in the woman's unhappy expression that none of these fates awaited Mariko. "I thank you before the spirits for bringing me these tidings."

Mariko's mistress made a warding gesture with her fingers. "Do not mention the devils to me, girl. I'm not some ignorant village brat who simply can't accept them for what they really are."

No, you're not, but we know what you did to get yourself exiled from Edo.

The woman's eyes flickered, but if she heard anything, she didn't acknowledge it. Mariko, of course, would never allow her features to betray her in that way; the difficulty lay in avoiding laughter.

"I'm sorry, Mistress."

"You should be. Now you need to do something with that hair. Such beautiful long hair, bedraggled because you refuse to tie it down." They fussed in front of a mirror until the older woman, whose grey-streaked locks were anything but beautiful, proclaimed herself satisfied. "Now come. We have a long way to go, and we do not want to be out after dark."

The woman led them on a roundabout path through the sparsely wooded lowlands. Any time they came upon a slight movement in the trees, or the soft sound of an animal scurrying away from them in the underbrush, the mistress would turn in the opposite direction, even if this meant having to climb over rubble strewn by the big tremor, the legendary event that had broken this small island off the mainland.

And yet, on the one occasion when they did come across a spirit, a dark cloud of smoke that looked almost solid in the path, the woman simply turned around, lips

86

pressed tightly together. Mariko was disappointed—she'd been hoping her beloved mistress would faint.

In much more time than was strictly necessary, the Samurai's palace came into view: a couple of large wood and paper houses in the classical style, surrounded by pleasing gardens and a not-so-pleasing wall with huge gaps in the stonework. The gate was open, and only when the path led over a bridge that crossed the stream in the garden, did the older woman relax. "Come girl. We have wasted enough time."

Mariko, still on the far side of the stream, nearly rebelled at the words. She wondered what the frightened mistress would do if her charge ran out into the sulfur fields where spirits roamed by the dozens. Would the woman follow, or would she take the only other honorable path open to her and throw herself down a fumarole?

This is not the moment to play games.

The young woman bowed her head and followed the mistress through the garden and up the steps leading to the front door. A guard who attempted to send them to the women's entrance was rebuffed.

"The Samurai will see this girl right now. That is his will."

The guard stood aside with an expression that conveyed that, though the decision could not be questioned, he would take enormous pleasure in executing them if the words proved false.

The two women entered the waiting room, where a long-whiskered attendant came over to greet them. Mariko was surprised by how foreign the interior of the traditional building looked. Books in exotic languages were laid on two shelves, a strange portrait of a round-eyed lady, pale and forbidding, adorned the back wall, and a long wooden musket hung on a specially reinforced paper panel.

She shouldn't have been surprised. The island, considered unholy since the tremor which had split it from the mainland, opened deep gashes in its fields, and filled its air with demons, was the only part of Nihon open to foreigners. Most of the villagers had some trinket or tool brought from some faraway port and given as a gift by sailors or exchanged for some service or good.

Perhaps what jarred was that the Samurai himself, that all-powerful emissary of Imperial Edo, should openly use his house to display so much that was alien. But it wasn't her place to question her betters.

The attendant rushed them through a single, flimsy door of traditional construction and, without further ado, they were in the noble presence. Both women bowed deeply.

"Please, we aren't in the Imperial court. You may face me."

Mariko looked up. This Samurai was a new one, arrived on the island some four months earlier, and the way he looked surprised her even more than his taste in decoration. Previous viceroys had been stern, dark-haired men, lean and menacing and clearly on the way to greater things than policing the empire's accursed island. This man, on the other hand seemed well past his prime to Mariko's young eye. His jowls hung to an almost obscene degree, and his hair was streaked with white.

She tried to imagine him riding to war, but was unable to imagine any horse large enough to carry him. Even his dark robes were unable to hide his girth. If he'd ever been one of the warriors of legend, that time was long past. At least his eyes seemed kind enough.

Mariko pulled her gaze away, settling it on a small jade figurine at a table by the Samurai's feet.

"We are here as requested," her mistress said.

"So I see, so I see." There was a hint of laughter in his voice. "Do you know why you are here, girl?"

"I am to be sent away."

"Yes, and do you know where?"

Mariko trembled. "To the pleasure cities. You would make me a *yujo*."

The Samurai's eyes opened wide. "No, no, no," he said. "Not a *yujo*, never a *yujo*. You have been trained, you have been educated, you have achievements. You will be *oiran*."

Mariko nearly snorted, but held her temper. She didn't know what *oiran* meant, but what difference would it make? She would only be concerned with the pleasure of others.

But it was the only way off the island for anyone who'd had the misfortune to be born there. The boys didn't even have that option.

Something of what she was thinking must have shown on her face, because the Samurai went on. "There is a difference, you know. An enormous difference. You will have an honored position among servants. From what the mistress informs me, you have the potential to earn respect for the women of Lesser Boso, to manage to convince Edo that you are not all mad."

Mariko heard the mistress take a sharp breath.

The Samurai went on. "You alone among the girls born before the breaking have shown yourself immune to the devil ghosts. Your mother must have been a remarkable woman."

"My mother was a fishwife who tore out her hair and threw herself into the sea to drown out the voice of the spirits."

The Samurai seemed nonplussed, both at the information and the way it was delivered: matter-of-factly, respectfully yet in much too forward a manner.

"Even so, you have survived the plague, and you alone can show the court that Lesser Boso has people who are not possessed. It is in your hands to make the travel restrictions disappear."

"But what if I am possessed? What if a spirit walks over the bridge inside me?"

He laughed at the village girl. "The devils cannot pass over the water. They are earth-devils, whose world was opened by the tremor, and the energy over the water sends them up—not only the dust we see, but also their essence—to be dispersed by the winds and destroyed. That is why streams surround this house, and also why your 'spirits' are unable to attack the people of the mainland."

"Then why are we kept apart from the empire?"

The old man sighed. "Even people at court fear what they do not understand. All they know is that the earth shook, destroying half of Edo. And when they recovered, there was an island where there had once been a peninsula. Imagine their shock when they learned that everyone on the island was mad, seeing ghosts and hearing their call."

"The ghosts are real."

"Yes. And so is the madness. There will be no safe passage to Edo until that is vanquished. Yours will not be the final step, but it will be the first. You will take that first step."

"What would happen if one of the devils crossed over?"

"No one knows for certain. Perhaps, being so far from its own place, it would shrivel and die. Perhaps it would be alone forever. And then again, maybe it would open the portal to thousands of its kind, hungry to drive the Imperial Capital mad and to feed on that madness, and to end the *Nihonjin* way of life. But let other minds worry about this. You must do your duty."

Mariko nodded, allowing herself to be led from the presence by her mistress, who was shaking with rage.

"You must never again speak to any noble in that way again. Not all of them have as much patience as the Samurai." She sounded bitter, and Mariko felt close to her for the first time. Could her exile have had something to do with this?

The attendant interrupted. "An honor guard will be waiting at the far end of the bridge. The young woman must cross immediately."

"But that cannot be. I cannot reach the bridge and return before sunset."

The man didn't even blink. "And yet it is your duty to lead the girl there and make certain her feet are set on the path."

Mariko could see the muscles moving in the mistress' jaw. Wordlessly, the other woman turned and stormed out of the foyer. Mariko followed.

The skies outside were painted red with sunset, but darkened also by cloud. As they crossed the garden, Mariko began, for the first time, to believe that everything she'd been told was true. Even as they crossed the wooden bridge over the stream, the first drop of a shower bounced off her nose.

Did you truly doubt the rain would be here?

The mistress made no comment, simply taking an uncharacteristically straight path to the bridge. Mariko struggled to keep up, while opening her umbrella. The mistress, oblivious, didn't even seem to notice that she was getting wet while her ward was dry. It was obvious that all the older woman wanted was to get back across the stream, to the Samurai's house and silence in her head.

They were making good time, carving through the open fields as if there were no such things as spirits, when the inevitable happened. The mistress, despite peering as hard as she could into the failing light, almost stumbled upon one of the clouds of floating smoke that betrayed the presence of a spirit.

The woman's demeanor cracked, and she jumped to one side with a shriek. Warned by this, Mariko saw the spirit in plenty of time. She could have avoided it easily.

But she didn't. She walked calmly into the space the spirit had occupied.

91

The mistress was upon her in an instant, fear of the supernatural overcome by the frantic realization that her precious cargo might have been damaged. Her hands traced the contours of Mariko's face while she repeated, over and over again, "Are you all right, are you all right?"

Mariko pretended confusion. "Yes, why?"

"There was a devil. You walked right into its arms. I saw it!"

"That's not possible. I would have seen it, would have felt something.

"But I saw it."

"It must have been a trick of the light." She took her mistress' hand and led her forward. "Come, it gets late."

Comforted by this, the mistress resumed her place in front of her. They arrived at the bridge without further incident, an unlikely pair: a young woman under a heavy waxed umbrella and a stately older woman, wide-eyed in the rain.

The bridge was a huge wooden affair of round logs and wooden boards. The guardhouse was thirty paces along its length, over the water, insuring that the earth-spirits could not molest the imperial troops stationed there.

A quick, curt goodbye at that guardhouse was all Mariko got on the moment in which she left everything she'd ever known behind. Her mistress turned back towards the comfortable confines of Lesser Boso, and the impulse to reach out to the receding woman was almost too strong to resist.

The guards removed the choice, however. They explained politely but firmly that she was expected on the far shore.

Mariko nodded numbly and walked out onto the boards, her umbrella rigidly upright in the slightly acidic rain that fell in this area, a product of the island's fumaroles. Her footfalls echoed dully as she advanced toward a vast world that was, she was certain, empty of anything she wanted.

It was important to hold the umbrella upright. Only that way could the carefully sealed canopy do its work, keep everything on the correct side of its surface. Holding it this way meant she was getting wet, but that didn't really matter.

The bridge, a few hundred paces long, took her an eternity to cross. The walk gave her the opportunity to remember every detail of her childhood, even those vaguely remembered sensations that were her only true memory of her mother. Did she have the right to keep others from knowing their mothers, even if, with that, they would become complete with the earth in a way they'd never known before?

Wet grass met her feet as the bridge ended. A small honor guard huddled under an awning some distance from the edge of the bridge, barely visible in the moonlight. Mariko noted that the structure didn't have a guard house on that side.

She stepped off the boards onto the wet grass. The guard had just noticed her, and she would have some moments before they got themselves organized. She shook the umbrella and nothing happened. She gave it another shake, fearful that all had been in vain.

A small cloud of dust motes, felt more than seen, dropped from the umbrella and coalesced into a smoky specter.

I have never felt such agony, but the barrier held me down against the energy. It is done.

Mariko said nothing, watching the guards approach, wondering if, even in their worst nightmares, they knew what was coming.

You have done well. You were always worthy. We thank you.

She finally managed to pull herself together enough to formulate a question, just as the cloud of smoke sank into its new shore.

"What's going to become of us? What's going to happen?" she whispered.

Something new.

###

About the Author

Gustavo Bondoni is an Argentine writer with over a hundred stories published in ten countries, in four languages, and was a winner in the National Space Society's "Return to Luna" Contest and the Marooned Award for Flash Fiction in 2008. His fiction has appeared in a Pearson High-school Test Cycle in the U.S., a Bundoran Press anthology, *The Rose & Thorn*, *Albedo One*, *The Best of Every Day Fiction*, and others.

His latest book, an ebook novella entitled *Branch*, was published by Wolfsinger Press in March 2014. He has also published two reprint collections, *Tenth Orbit and Other Faraway Places* (2010) and *Virtuoso and Other Stories* (2011, Dark Quest Books). *The Curse of El Bastardo* (2010) is a short fantasy novel. His website is at www.gustavobondoni.com.ar, and his blog is located at http://bondo-ba.livejournal.com/.

*****〜〜〜*****

The Perfection of the Steam-Powered Armour

by Adria Laycraft

Perfection. Nothing less would do.

Jin adjusted the final gear 2.7 mm closer to its partner, and tightened the valve to allow just the right amount of steam. A turn of the tool made each connection move in harmony, and he smiled at the precision of it. Then he prepared the final piece, the connection that would allow the fighter's *neijin* energy to flow into the workings, melding warrior and machine into a deadly combination.

A noise startled him, and his hand loosened before he could recover. The heavy wrench fell, as if in slow motion, and knocked against the lower mechanism before he could even cry out his dismay.

The alignment, gone. The gear, dented.

This would set him back hours, and General Li Jiang could arrive at any time.

His roar of anger emerged even before he turned to see his son Wen cowering by the door.

"Stupid boy! How many times must I tell you to stay away while I work? It must be flawless, and now it is ruined." His words flowed out before he could consider the effect on his son. "The General will come, and find you at fault."

Tears welled in the ten-year-old's eyes, serving only to fuel his fury.

"Stay out until it is done!"

The boy fled, and Jin blinked, his rage gone in an instant. He sighed, shook off the regret. "The boy must learn." But Jin knew his son was no warrior. "It is my own fault, my own shame," he muttered. "The only way is to please the General with my invention, so that he will spare both my son and me from the life of a soldier."

He undid the damaged gear and started again. Each gear in the line had to be loosened to free up the room to add the new replacement, and by the time they all lined up again, Jin's jaw hurt from grinding his teeth.

"It is done."

He looked about him, as if awakening, realizing how his work made him at one with Enlightenment. He stepped back and studied the suit of armour. Alarmed by the smudges on the bright metal, he snatched up a rag and began to polish his greatest accomplishment.

Again he did not hear the approaching footsteps, lost as he was in his feverish work. When his awareness awoke, he turned too quickly, only to be pinned to his knees by a rough hand, his head forced forward into a bow.

The shoes of the Emperor's official uniform passed by his nose, and he saw his creation in his mind's eye as General Li Jiang must see it for himself now. A fighter's suit like none other, made to enhance every move, every reflex, every strike. If the wearer could channel their *neijin ch'i* and focus that life force into the suit, the steam would power the gears, creating an unbeatable soldier.

"Does it work?"

Jin spoke to the floor. "I have only just finished. All that remains is to test it. One of your fine warriors—"

"It must work perfectly, for anyone." The words cut in over his, and his heart stuttered. "That was your promise."

"I am no warrior, my lord."

His laughter was echoed by that of his men. "While you would make a fine test subject, we have brought an even better one."

A small sound, familiar and gut-wrenching, made Jin lift his head. There, dragged along by two warriors, was his son. Tears leaked down the boy's face, shaming him and his father. Sick fear shot Jin to his feet before he could think better of it.

"He is only a child!"

The General snorted his distaste. "You have babied him, and he is nearly a man. This will make it the best kind of test." The General stopped right before him, and Jin dropped his gaze, choking on the stench of power.

His helplessness stank even worse.

"You claimed it would make any man into a fearsome warrior, yes?"

Jin nodded. *If they could channel their neijin, their internal power.* But he dared not argue. Men had died for less.

"Show me."

A Wushu warrior entered the workshop, while Jin strapped the armour onto his pale son. His hands trembled at each buckle, and he fought to calm his fear to ensure that each pressure point was covered, each gear linked, each valve set just so.

It must be perfect.

"Use your *neijin* as I taught you, let it flow from the Universe through you," he whispered. "Choose the *qiang*—it is longer and lighter than a sword—and think of the Tai Chi we do each morning. Think of sweeping the stones, and let the *qiang* become a simple broomstick. Then add the movements. If your inner energy flows, it will engage the steam, power the suit, and make each move a powerful strike instead of the peaceful movements we are used to."

Wen hiccupped. "I can't."

"You must," he said through clenched teeth. Jin wanted to scream at him. Didn't the boy see? If he failed, then Jin failed, and he would be sent off to fight like a normal soldier. Within a few years, if not months, he'd be dead. Then they would come for Wen, force him to follow in his bloody footsteps.

97

Jin gripped the shoulders of the suit and gave Wen a little shake. "The suit will make you powerful," he said, forcing Wen to look at him. "Do not shame me."

They emerged into the courtyard beyond the workshop. The General's warrior swung his gleaming *jian*, the sword's edge flashing in the clear spring air. Wen stood opposite him, his metal-encased hand clenching his *qiang* as if the spear was a lifeline and he was drowning.

The warrior, all in black and with his face covered, swept his foot back and raised his free hand. A pose of readiness. Jin felt sweat trickle down his back. He had faith in his invention, but its workings were meant for men, not his son.

Wen still stood stork-like, his eyes showing white all around. He did not even settle into opening stance.

The boy was frozen with fear.

The warrior lunged forward, and Wen stumbled backwards with a shriek. The General and his men laughed, enjoying the show for the moment.

"Wen, white crane preening wing," Jin ordered.

His voice cut through the laughter and reached the boy. Out of habit, Wen bent slightly, rotated his foot, and his arms moved the spear just so. His hands came together, then apart, and the spear spun, looking dangerous. Little puffs of steam leaked free into the cool air.

The warrior leapt forward to strike.

"Hand strums the *pipa*!"

Wen shifted his weight back, his hands came up, and the staff deflected the sword's strike.

The laughing faltered into silence.

The black warrior gave a grunt of displeasure, and lunged forward again.

"Grasping bird's tail," Jin cried, and Wen pivoted as his hands shifted, the staff spinning impossibly fast. Steam hissed free, and the blade sliced the air where Wen once stood. Wen caught the staff, and thrust it into the warrior's gut.

"Single whip!"

And, with comprehension dawning on his face, Wen drew his left foot, heel first then toe, balanced and ready, as his weight shifted and the staff swung in a beautiful arc. . .

. . . that stopped, and Jin heard the gears grind to a halt.

The warrior threw up his arm to shield a blow that never came, and in the instance that the realization hit him, let his fist fly and connect with Wen's face, snapping the boy's head back with a sickening crunch.

"No!"

Jin ran, too slow to break the fall, and dropped to his knees beside his son. Relief flooded him when he saw that Wen, bleeding and broken, still breathed.

The finely slippered feet of a General of the Emperor again graced his lowered vision.

"It has promise." The words held a weight of begrudging respect. A long pause followed, and Jin wondered what torture would come down on him next.

"You have told me of your wish for better *guanxi*, Jin Yong," the General said. "I can raise you to a much higher social standing, with the social connections you need for success. But I can only do this if I am a success."

Another pause, giving Jin time to remember how badly he craved great *guanxi*. Such status would raise him above the level of commoner, and he would no longer be required to serve as a foot soldier in the Emperor's ill-fated war.

"You have one day to try again. Failure means death."

Failure in this meant eventual death as a soldier anyway. Jin saw his son's breath bubble through the blood pouring out his nose. He had no choice but to succeed. He rose and bowed, perfect, formal. "I accept your words, my lord."

Once they were gone Jin helped Wen to his feet, disengaged the armour, and washed his bloodied face with gentle hands. Wen did not cry out, nor complain about the pain. He kept his gaze downcast. When he was free of the machine, he stood to one side, head hung low, while Jin inspected the armour.

He could find no faulty valve, no jammed gear.

Jin went to stand before Wen and waited. His presence forced the boy to look up and face him.

"You stopped before you could strike the General's warrior," Jin said. "It was not the fault of my machine."

"True." Some grim determination narrowed Wen's eyes. His mouth gaped, his nose unable to pass air for all the blood. "I have no wish to fight."

Jin stared, his mind stalled and jammed as sure as any misplaced gear. Wen held his gaze.

"What of your honor, your loyalty to your country?" Jin finally said. "What of filial piety?"

"Filial piety is not just loyalty to one's country," Wen said, his voice high and soft, but sure. "It is also a way to ensure a peaceful family and society. I have heard what you say about this war. There is no virtue in proving I can fight, machine or no machine."

Jin regarded his son with new eyes. He heard his dead wife's voice echo through his memories. "You demand respect from him, but you show none," his wife would always say.

Even still, Jin felt that Wen did not understand the situation. "I respect your quest for virtue, Son," he said, and hoped Wen knew he meant it. "However, if I do not complete this machine to the Emperor's satisfaction, I will be killed, and you will be forced to fight, virtue or no. You will have no choice."

"There is always a choice." Again Jin heard echoes of the boy's mother in Wen's words.

"A fine sentiment," Jin said, his patience waning. "Tell me, what would you choose?"

Wen ignored the sarcasm. He lifted his head and regarded his father. The look held a challenge.

"We could leave, travel north and west, live a peaceful life in the country."

"And slave over the land our whole lives?"

Wen nodded. "Better to be at One with the land than at One with killing and death."

Jin stepped back, shock flooding his body. His creation, while perfect, served war and hatred, violence and, yes, death. His machine served the very things he ached to avoid.

At first he thought he could not honor his son's dream and his own at the same time. Now he saw that his path only betrayed his dreams. He had deceived himself.

He did not want to leave his workshop and the perfection of creation. But the world was too much full of wonderful chaos to be perfect.

"Come," he said to Wen. "We must hurry if we will be away before the General returns."

Wen's eyes widened. "I will pack our things." He ran headlong for the doorway, but stopped there, turning back with dismay on his face. "Will you leave the machine?"

"Yes."

Jin saw the disappointment on his son's face-- disappointment in him. "We cannot take it, or they will hunt for us," Jin explained. "If we leave them a working machine, there is a chance they will let us go our way."

Wen looked ready to cry again. "They will take your design and make more, yes?"

Jin nodded.

"And these machines—will they make the Emperor's army strong enough that the war will end sooner?"

He was too wise, his boy.

"No. It would only make it bloodier," Jin said, his voice soft. "The Emperor, fueled by my machine's perfection, would only find new enemies to fight, more lands to conquer."

Jin went to his son and placed a hand on his shoulder. "Today you have proven yourself a man, Wen. You have shown me that you possess the deepest wisdom, and perfect honour. Go gather our things. . . quickly now."

Wen hurried away, and Jin turned to his creation. What could he do? If he destroyed the machine, the General would send men in every direction after them. If he left it, he became the thing he hated.

Then he knew. With sure movements, he set to work, tightening this gear, adjusting this fitting. It had to be just perfect. Nothing less would do.

When Wen returned, two large bundles bending his back, Jin waved him over.

"Put it on."

Wen stepped back, shaking his head.

"Please, just trust me," Jin said, tired now. "I have to know I got it right."

So for the second time that day Jin tightened straps and ensured a good fit of his steam-powered armour over his son's body. Then, taking up a staff and tossing another over to Wen, he jumped to attack.

Wen stopped the strike.

Jin smiled. "Now strike me." Wen's mouth tightened, and Jin saw the protest forming. "Quickly! If we are to be gone when the General returns. . . "

Wen spun his staff, little puffs of steam clouding the air. He stepped closer. Gripped the staff. Swung.

The strike stopped a hair's breadth from Jin's forehead.

"That was not me," cried Wen, his eyes wide. "I swear by every god, Father, I did not make it stop!"

"I know, Son. I made it so, just as you taught me. And now, it is truly perfect."

###

About the Author

Adria Laycraft is a grateful member of IFWA and a proud survivor of the Odyssey Writers Workshop. She co-edited *Urban Green Man*, which launched in August of 2013, and is nominated for an Aurora Award. Look for her stories in FAE, Tesseracts 16, Neo-opsis, On-Spec, James Gunn's Ad Astra, Hypersonic Tales, DKA Magazine, and In Places Between. Author of *Be a Freelance Writer Now*, Adria lives in Calgary with her husband and son.

*****~~~~~*****

Abbreviated Epics

Assault On the Summit

by Daniel Coble

To: Gen. Roger Naismith
<rznaismith@specialcomintgroup7.mil>
From: Col. Armando Godoy
<asgodoy@usarmy.mil>
Subject: Historical Data Possibly
Relating to Ongoing Projects
x-encryption-protocol: non-correspond-trinary-4096-b

General Naismith,

Please find attached the scanned contents of a bundle of letters found last week by a South Korean climbing team on the southern approach to Mt. Nending, Nepal. The documents were in a wrapped bundle under some rocks at an altitude of 16,400 feet. Provenance is still being confirmed, but some aspects of this unsent correspondence may be of interest to us, in particular the mention of a "luminescent crystalline latticework." No such artifact has been found near this site, but if any trace of it can be located, it may shed light on the xenomorphic fragments found in 2010 on Mt. Cotopaxi in Ecuador. Some parts of Polk's accounts may be simply the result of altitude sickness - particularly the face-peeling portion - but I thought you would want to see them ASAP in any case.

Regards,
Armando

...

To Sir Manfred Ottsworth, Chairman, Committee for Exploration

The Royal Society of England for Improving Natural Knowledge

16th May, 1871

Esteemed Professor Ottsworth,

I write today with the utmost enthusiasm and the solid expectation of achieving an even more scientifically and historically significant expeditionary success than I had previously predicted. The journey from Calcutta through Kathmandu and finally to the Sagarmatha Plateau has proceeded splendidly, my equipment remains in perfect order, and I am on the verge of securing the services of several skilled, robust, and doughty indigenous guides, drawn from a people called "Sherpas," who will aid my ascent to the summit, bearing on their strong backs all of the scientific sampling apparatus, food, and climbing gear needed for the final stages of the journey. I must again thank the Royal Society for their generous support of this historic endeavour.

Ebullient regards,
Prof. Charles Morgan Polk

...

To Mary Louisa Polk
Old Ford, London
17th May, 1871

My Dearest Mary,

I must confess to you, my heart, that I seem to have discovered not so much the gateway to scientific glory and social reputation, as the dreary outskirts of Hell itself. Or perhaps those of Hel, the icy, Nordic world of the undistinguished dead, because even at the relatively modest altitudes at which I now sojourn, the cold is unrelenting.

The village in which I'm now stuck, called "Phurumba" by the surly and thick-skulled locals, is one of a scattering of such settlements on the plateau from which the final stages of my expedition must launch. The indigenes are unfriendly in the extreme, so closed in their countenances and so mired in a reflexive and hateful reserve as to behave toward outsiders in a manner which can only be called "cruel."

Ethnologically the region's society is peculiar, based on the almost-unheard-of practice of polyandry, with each stout and weathered woman having two or more husbands, since the environment is so marginal, and their economic abilities so stunted, that no single man can support a wife and children. This may explain the obnoxious attitude of the men here. Frankly, Mary, no one will say a damned word to me. It's only by waving silver coins in their faces that I can persuade one to give me a disgusting bowl of unsavoury stew, and only through threats of physical force that I can induce any to allow me to lodge under their roof for the night.

I am mostly recovered from the intestinal flux I acquired on my arrival months ago in Calcutta, but the altitude and the inferior foodstuffs upon which I am subsisting leave me in a continual state of vague nausea and de-energetic malaise. I hope that I can make a few of these swarthy bastards serve as my guides and bearers soon, for I fear that before long I may lack the strength even to make the final climb.

Of course, assuming that I succeed, this will be not just an adventure of epic effort, but one of soaring scientific achievement. But I admit to becoming dispirited in the face of the difficulties presented by this bleak landscape and its nearly subhuman inhabitants.

I hope you and the girls are in good health and enjoying a delightful spring. Give Penny and Hester my love.

> Yours, adoringly but discouragedly,
> Charles

...

To Professor Ellard Drinker Standish
University of Cambridge, Faculty of Geography and Natural Philosophy

9th June, 1871

My dear Professor Standish,

I hardly know how to report to you on the complications with which this venture has continued to surprise me. The long journey here to the Himalayas was, as you predicted, much more grueling than I had thought. Simply bringing my supplies up to the Sagarmatha plateau became appallingly expensive, and involved the financial lubrication of more deceitful, grasping local officials than I would have believed could possibly even exist in this part of the world.

Further, acquiring local guides and pack-carriers for the actual climb proved to be an achievement more Herculean than perhaps even my impending victory over the peak of Nending. I had no success in recruiting from among any of the dismal villages that dot this plateau like the pock-marks of a disease, but finally was able to hire two guides who arrived quite unexpectedly from another area entirely. In fact, they seem to be as ignorant as I of the local dialect, but like me they command enough Urdu and Tibeto-Burman phrases to make themselves understood. The two men, named "Norn" and "Shambul" as near as I can tell, have proven most agreeable and competent, and we have already made our way from the plateau up and across the glacial slopes, over the Khumbu Pass, and partway up the southern ridge of Mt. Nending herself. I am extremely optimistic, and count myself very fortunate to have secured the aid of these two sturdy men.

Meeting them was quite serendipitous. They appeared one evening in the village of Phurumba where I was ensconced, apparently having heard that a European climber was looking for guides. The sour Phurumbans were only too happy to be rid of me, and put me in contact with them straight away.

I am as yet unclear on their ethnic origins. They said that they were Sherpas, but a local man whose hatred of me is somewhat less than the local average told me emphatically that they are not. They are no taller than the locals, but move with a fluidity and sprightly agility utterly unlike the plodding gait and clumsy gestures of the people of the plateau.

Many of the locals seemed, oddly, to be somewhat afraid of Norn and Shambul, and at first I attributed it to the villagers' apparently congenital xenophobia, but now I sneak myself toward the suspicion that my guides may engage in esoteric religious practices that violate local taboos, or at least are strange enough to provoke fear. I haven't directly witnessed many of their rituals or observances, because both men are quite furtive about them and only perform them when they believe that I cannot see. But I have seen a couple of odd practices which I think are intriguing enough that an anthropological paper or two may follow the geographic and geological ones I will undoubtedly publish on my return to England.

One of their activities has to do with small, glassy spheres that they carry. Each is about the size of an apricot, and they appear to be dark in color and oblately spheroid in shape, like some of the paperweights that Mary collects. They are so highly polished that even in the dim light of early evening they appear almost to glow with an inner light. I have twice seen Norn engage in the ritual practice associated with the stones: he will secretively extract his from an inner pocket or pouch, hold it on his palm, near his mouth, and whisper rapidly at it for some minutes. Periodically he will pause in his sibilant discourse, hold the stone to his ear, and act as though he is actually listening to replies from whatever god or spirit he believes dwells within.

The other practice resembles a form of Yoga, although of course we are more than five hundred miles from the nearest area in which Yoga is known to be practised. If it is Yogic in nature, it is certainly quite different from any such discipline that I have observed. Here is what they do: each man will from time to time wander some distance away, and settle in a place concealed from camp by rocky outcroppings or steep slopes, much as though he intended to relieve his bladder. There he will put his hands on the ground, feet still flat, and stretch and undulate his body in the most remarkable manner. It is as though they were performing an extreme version of the "dog" and "cat" poses of Indian Yoga, but with a flexibility and liquidity that gives the illusion of their bodies waving and undulating in a manner which would be anatomically quite impossible. It is a mesmerizing sight, and I hope to see more of it. Indeed, I very much hope that I can gain their trust to a degree that will lead them to speak openly of all of these rituals.

I must stop writing now, as my lamp oil is burning low, and I must fold up my desk in preparation for tomorrow's travels. Of course, there will undoubtedly be time for me to add to this letter later, long before I reach anywhere from which I can post it to you.

With warm and high-spirited regards,
Charles Polk

...

To Mary Louisa Polk
Old Ford, London
14th June, 1871

Beloved Mary,

I write to you tonight in a most agitated state, and I apologize if my words seem alarming in any way, but I must put my suspicions and concerns down on paper, even if they will have been proven quite groundless by the time I send this to you.

I have come to suspect that my two guides, Norn and Shambul, who initially seemed to be so helpful and agreeable, may be working against me, for reasons unknown. Perhaps I am merely in a condition of disturbed spirits due to exhaustion and thin air, and perhaps nothing nefarious is going on, but the signs of trouble are striking.

On three occasions now, supplies have gone missing. I do not mean a bit of dried corn or salt beef stolen as a treat by one of the men, but whole bundles and boxes of materials. The entirety of my wheat flour, precious to me even in its larva-infested state, vanished without a trace. Both of my telescopes—both of them!—have disappeared from within my equipment crate. And yesterday morning, upon rising, I found that two of my three coils of highest-grade climbing rope are gone as well. The two men deny any knowledge of these miraculous disappearances, and I can see no way that they could be concealing any of these things on their persons,

111

but the bare facts are incontrovertible. These crucial items are gone, and I did not dispose of them myself.

What reason my guides might have for stealing my supplies and equipment and hurling them into the void of a steep, Himalayan gorge I cannot imagine. Does it have to do with their secret and mysterious religious faith? I have no idea. And more importantly, I have no idea what they will do next. If they expect to dissuade me from continuing by depriving me of food and tools, they are doomed to disappointment. But if they are truly determined to prevent my success, how far might they go? Might they conspire to murder me? Although it would be little help against a cut rope or even a sharp shove over a precipice, I have taken to carrying my revolver, loaded, in the pocket of my parka at all times.

Of course, you know better than anyone how contrary I can be. Any effort to keep me from achieving the summit of Nending will only make me more determined to reach it. Indeed, the stronger my suspicions of wrongdoing by my guides become, the more I start to hope that the fantastic reports of what I might find on the peak might have some truth to them.

As I told you so long ago, legends from across the region say that a fabulous and ancient temple hides among the clouds atop Mt. Nending. Drunken Gurkhas in the pubs of Kathmandu will happily relate to anyone their absurd ravings that the Nepalese-Tibetan war of the 1850s was about control of that temple itself, and thus about access to a race of magnificent demigods imagined to dwell there, waiting to pass on their unearthly wisdom to any mortal who proves himself worthy by making the climb. I can reassure you that I'm not so thin-air addled that I believe such tales, but the treachery of my two companions makes me wonder if there might not at least be some ruins of a lost civilization there. Mary, just think what a grand climax to my adventure that would be!

Missing you more than I can possibly say,
Charles

…

To Professor Ellard Drinker Standish
University of Cambridge, Faculty of Geography and Natural Philosophy

15th June, 1871

Ellard, my note to you must be brief, for I fear my life is in danger, and I may not have time to write much. Of course, if I'm correct then I'll likely never have an opportunity to send this. But I may be worrying unnecessarily. In any event, there is much more to tell than I can record at this time. I'll put it this way: my epic adventure will soon either be cut short or explode into a series of discoveries that will positively concuss the academic establishment, revolutionizing not only our geographical knowledge, but also the sciences of ethnology, archaeology, and even zoology. Astronomy as well, perhaps. There is so much to relate. I pray that I will be permitted to do so.

Regards,
Charles

…

To Mary Polk
Old Ford, London
17th June, 1871

Dearest Mary,

The things I have seen! I cannot begin to explain the wonderment I have felt at my most recent discoveries, and indeed my hands are shaking so violently from cold and respiratory exhaustion that I cannot write at length at all. But I have to share, or at least imagine that I am sharing, some of this with you, my beloved.

Norn and Shambul have taken no hostile action against me, and no further loss of supplies or equipment has occurred. But that does not take away my suspicions about these two, so I have been perseverant and stealthy in my surveillance of their actions. And as a result I have witnessed an occurrence more amazing than I could ever have imagined.

Yesterday afternoon I followed Norn up a trackless, icy slope, ending up on a rocky saddle perhaps five hundred feet higher than our camp. At this altitude such ascensions are severe in their effects, and I could barely breathe at all as I hid behind a boulder to observe him. As I watched, he stood upon a flat rock, pulled out his little spirit-stone, and began whispering to it. Within moments, as though by magic, the most amazing structure formed about him, as if congealing out of the rarefied atmosphere itself. It was red and radiant and complex, a cylinder made of a luminescent crystalline latticework, like some exotic, glowing web of delicate, translucent coral. This scintillating form surrounded Norn, and suddenly, he was gone, the cylinder with him. I tried to believe that he had suddenly fallen off an edge out of sight, but he had not. He vanished instantaneously before my unblinking eyes. I have no explanation. I cannot report to my colleagues at the Royal Society until I have understood and documented these wonders, but when I do report, I do not believe that I exaggerate when I say that I shall become the most celebrated man in England.

Lovingly,
Charles

...

18th June, 1871

Mary, I will write this in the hope that by hiding my letters I can ensure that you will eventually receive them. I wish that I could conceal my notebooks as well, but those are in my pack at the camp, and I cannot get to them without being exposed. I do not believe that I shall ever see your lovely face again, and for this I am deeply sorry.

This morning, as I awoke, I saw Norn and Shambul starting back down the mountain, carrying everything but my tent and sleeping roll. I could not let them stop me so close to my goal, so I ran to stand before them, drew my revolver and ordered them to halt. I told them they could go, but not with my possessions. Shambul raised his hand as though to strike me, and I fired once, directly at his head.

The bullet entered his forehead, but seemed to have little effect other than tearing the skin. Then he reached up to the wound, and employing it as a starting-hole, used his fingers to peel away the entirety of his face, as though it were no more than a layer of damp clay! Beneath it was what I can only call another face. It was smooth and pale, with numerous glowing eyes like those of a spider. I screamed like a child, and ran. I have taken refuge behind some boulders, but they cannot have failed to see where I have gone, and will doubtless be upon me shortly. I will hide these letters and pray. I love you, Mary.

###

About the Author

Daniel Coble develops Web applications for his corporate masters during the day, and writes like a maniac in the dark of night. He lives in southern California with his wife and two daughters, where he enjoys painting and 3,425 other hobbies.

*****~~~~~*****

Fortunate Son

by Steve Coate

"But I don't want you to go."

Freya picked up the round shield that had been passed down to her by her father. It was constructed of good, solid oak and had held strong through the generations. "Silly, Bjorn," she admonished her child. "You are unhappy when I am home, and you are unhappy when I am gone." She turned to face him. "You are an unhappy boy."

Bjorn pouted. "I am not a boy. I am a man."

She smiled and strode to her son of twelve seasons. "Soon enough, Bjorn." She ruffled his hair with one hand. "Soon enough."

He swatted at her hand, but she was too quick. "I don't want to go to Aunt Yrsa's. I am old enough to care for myself."

Freya stood before her son. "Perhaps it is your Aunt Yrsa who needs caring for. Ever since Uncle Heimer fell in battle, she has dwelled by her lonesome. She would benefit greatly from your company." She smiled. "It would be the adult thing to do."

Bjorn's chest puffed out. "Then I shall do it." He let the air out of his nose in a blast. "How long will you be away?"

Freya checked the sword in its scabbard for the hundredth time. "I know not. We raid the lands to the east. The journey will take at least a day by boat, and I cannot say how long we will be in those lands before we return."

Bjorn examined his feet. When he spoke his voice was smaller than before. "I don't like it when you leave. Father left too, and he never came back."

Freya knelt and took her son by the arms as she looked him in his upraised eyes. "Your father was a great warrior, Bjorn. He did not want to leave you. It was his time to go to Valhalla. We will all be called to Valhalla one day, provided we live and die well. On that day, we will all be together again, feasting in the great hall of the gods. Until that day, we must live well. Sometimes that means doing things we would rather not. Do you understand this?"

Bjorn searched his mother's eyes. Then he nodded. "Yes, mother."

She gave his arms a reassuring squeeze. "Good."

Freya stood and strode to the door of their domicile. She held a hand out to her son. "Come. I shall walk with you to Yrsa's."

...

She was the last to reach the pier. All the other warriors were gathered, breast beating and jostling one another, as men do. "Freya," called one. "So glad you could join us. Have you finished wiping the snot from your boy's nose, then?"

This drew guffaws from the other warriors assembled before the longboat. A couple steps closer and she was able to identify the man. She cupped one hand and held it up before her as she continued her approach. "I saved some for you, Geir, because I know you are a warrior of discerning taste."

The others fell to laughing once more as Geir slapped Freya's empty hand away. Even Iarl, the raid leader, joined in the mirth. "This is your first raid since taking up the family life, is it not, Freya?" Geir turned his head from side to side to ensure he had the attention of the other warriors. "It is good that a woman accompanies us. I can think of a good use for a woman."

His pelvic thrusts served as a visual aid, in case no one else caught the gist of his jape.

"And what is that, Geir?" Freya moved to the side, near Geir, whose ale-laced breath she could smell from where she stood as he laughed with the others. "Do you

118

require maternal discipline?" She drew her sword, swinging her arm wide and then back at Geir, whose eyes had gone wide. "I am adept at administering a good spanking." The flat of her sword swatted Geir's rear end. "Should you step out of line."

She sheathed her sword as the warriors around her roared with laughter. Some of them were beginning to tear up from the exertion. Once things had calmed down, Iarl called for silence. "If everyone is done playing, then let's board and be away. The Slav coffers await."

Freya made sure to stay well away from Geir as she took an oar alongside Leiknir. She and Leiknir soon got into a rhythm, and she remembered the monotony of the action from her time as a shield maiden. The eel-skin drum beat out a tempo that called the oars to the water under the skilled hands of the Northmen. The motion of the oars and the craft cutting through the sea calmed her and allowed her mind to move to other things.

Today was the first since Eldgrim died in battle that Bjorn had ever asked her to stay at home. In the past, he had asked her why she did not go on raids with other warriors and shield maidens. Until today, her answer was always the same. "I must stay here to care for you and make sure that you grow to be a big, strong warrior."

Often, this was enough to satisfy the boy. As he grew older, so did his curiosity. "You mean I am holding you back?" he would ask. "You could be a famed shield maiden with songs sung and tales told in her honor, were it not for me?"

"No!" she would always answer. "A thousand times, no." She would crouch down on her haunches to meet the boy's eyes and take him by the arms. "You are a gift, Bjorn, not a hindrance. I have already killed many of our enemies, before you were born. Ask anyone in the village, and they will tell you this is so." What she did not say was that a shield maiden was only as good as her last raid. And her last raid was many seasons past, as the warriors and shield maidens in the village never tired of reminding her.

The truth was that she was afraid. Not of battle, nor falling to violence. Freya feared leaving her only son. Theirs was a warrior culture. She had seen more than a few children raised by extended family, or in some cases, by villagers who were of no relation, because the child's adult family members had all died in battle. This was not a fate she wished upon her son.

But like the fierce and savage Slavs, fear could only be conquered by facing it head on. And now was the proper time. Whether she returned home with plunder, or on her shield, she would be a heroine in the eyes of her son. That was all that mattered.

...

They made landfall the following afternoon. After securing the boat, the raiding party moved east, crossing a log bridge, then moving through the trees until a village came into sight. Geir fingered the haft of his iron axe. "Do we attack?"

"No," replied Iarl. "Save your blood lust."

In time, the sun dipped below the horizon and was replaced by mother moon, whose light winked from behind passing clouds. A great fire burned in the center of the village, around which the Slavs gathered and ate a communal meal. "Now?" prompted Geir.

"Soon." Iarl remained seated on the leaf-strewn ground.

More time passed. Several of the villagers were sleeping around the remains of the dwindling fire, the other Slavs having retreated to their domiciles. Iarl stood and brushed the leaves and dirt from his leggings and the seat of his pants. He drew his sword, iron glinting in the light of the moon's pale kiss. "Now."

...

The screams of the Slavs crowded the night air as the raiding party, efficient and swift, cut them down at every turn. Those who could manage it fled into the anonymous folds of the night. When their foes were either dead or gone, Iarl charged the others with plundering the village, and they each set about their tasks.

Once the raiders had all filled their sacks with the riches of the Slavs, they regrouped and headed back up the hill to the forest to retrace their path to the boat. After crossing the bridge, Iarl called a halt to the party. A look across the bridge to the forest beyond evidenced the Slavs were less than willing to part with their treasure. A party of Slav warriors approached. Iarl turned to the others.

"We must get the treasure back to the ship. With its weight slowing us, they will catch us easily. We need a volunteer to hold the bridge and give the rest of us time to load the ship."

The others took a moment to consider. They all understood what it was that Iarl was asking. Freya let her sack of plunder drop to the ground.

"I will do it." She unsheathed her sword and rapped it twice against her shield as she met Iarl's gaze.

Iarl nodded at the woman and reached for the sack, pulling back his hand as Geir beat him to the chore. Geir hauled the sack over one shoulder and looked to Freya. "Bjorn is a fortunate son to have a mother so valiant."

Freya showed Geir her back so the man would not see the tears her son's name had evoked. She heard him turn and join the others, as their footfalls indicated their flight to the boat. She moved to the center of the bridge, clanging her sword against her shield to taunt the enemy.

She would give her son the tale of bravery that he had always desired, even though it meant she would never see him again. As the Slavs advanced, the warrior woman set her feet and raised her sword high, a ferocious battle cry ripping forth from her lips.

###

About the Author

Steve Coate is a speculative fiction writer who lives in sunny South Florida, where he struggles daily for dominion of the keyboard with his possessive tabby, Bigby. His short fiction has also appeared in Plasma Frequency Magazine and *Stupefying Stories: SHOWCASE* among other publications. For a full bibliography, visit coaterack.blogspot.com. Follow Steve on Twitter @stevecoate for updates on his fiction. Readers can also drop him a line at stevecoate11@gmail.com.

*****~~~~~*****

Odin on the Tree

by Jo Walton

Light flick, leaf flash
Words well, wonder…

Light flick, leaf flash,
Words well, wonder…

I wonder what wisdom I came here to gain
In this flicker of light, on this tree, in this pain,
As my sacrifice made to myself in my pride,
Hung here and given whole.

Light fails, blood price
Death, war, fire, ice.

Here is memory's price, that I killed and I lied
And I pondered death's price as I lived, I denied
The dominion of death for the races I shaped
And gave my breath to draw them through the
dark.

Throne, price, hang tree,
Fire, ice, you, me

(Mystery, mystery, teach us our history)

So the visions I see are the price of a throne
Where I hang from this gallows and always alone,
With the runes I can read and my worlds lying free
With no more mystery.

Ash tree, world fruit,

Leaf, light, well root.

And the sight that I gain is the price of an eye
As the wind shakes the branches and passes me by
And the raven-swift rustlings of thought and desire
Become the price of all that I require.

Times branch, winds blow
Words well, you know.

I am I as I hang in the heart of this tree
And there are no directions in all I can see
And I bind myself fast to the duty I owe
With all my mastery.

Suns rise, wind shakes
Dream sons, hope wakes.

No up and no down and no start and no end
And the worlds are all mine, with no equal, no
friend,
Just the dream of a father that sons may surpass
And the hope to guide them forward, through the
dark.

Nine worlds, ice, sire,
Best worlds, desire

I shaped the nine worlds from the wreck of the war
And the fragments of all that had stood there
before
And I stood as the father of all I had made
Alone as I have stayed.

Light comes, wind near,
Words well, dreams fear.

Odin on the Tree

With my strength and my cunning and all I can lend

And the wisdom of runes that no price can amend
And the choice that I made when I bound myself here

They all lie bare before me, free and clear.

Fire, ice, wait breath
Wind knows, life, death
Wonder, I wonder, I wonder…

For nine nights open-eyed with the Norns and the tree

In the wind, until everything's speaking to me
And the future lies open, with my mystery
But bound by prophecy.
So I dream of a fire to make me feel warm
And a friend who would stand by my side in the storm

And a son who could teach me a new way to be,
As my wonders keep revolving, through the dark.

(Built such wonders, and lost them again to the dark)

###

About the Author

Jo Walton has published ten novels, three poetry collections, and an essay collection, with another two novels due out in 2015. Her most recent novel is *My Real Children*. She won the John W. Campbell Award for Best New Writer in 2002, the World Fantasy Award in 2004 for *Tooth and Claw*, and the Hugo and Nebula awards in 2012 for *Among Others*. She comes from Wales, but lives in Montreal, where the food and books are much better.

She writes science fiction and fantasy, reads a lot, talks about books, and eats great food. She plans to live to be ninety-nine and write a book every year.

Jo wrote this as the first stretch goal for the Sassafrass Sundown kickstarter in May 2013. Reprinted with permission of the author.

*****~~~~*****

Refusing the Call

by Elliotte Rusty Harold

Bang! Bang! Bang!

Jonathan stumbled out of the shower and reached for a towel. "I'm coming! Hold your horses." He knotted the towel around his waist and hurried across his apartment. Why did the super always come when he was in the shower? Was it leaking into Mrs. Delacroix's apartment again?

By the time Jonathan reached his front door, the towel had started to slip. He tried to hold it up with one hand as he threw the door open. "What is so urgent that you can't—" and then he stopped, momentarily rendered speechless by the sight not of the rotund Ukrainian superintendent he was expecting but rather a robed and bearded wizard, near seven feet tall (if you included the pointy hat), holding a gnarled staff in his left hand, a staff he had apparently been using to practice the cannon solo from the 1812 Overture on Jonathan's front door.

"Jonathan Harris, I have come to fetch you on a quest of most urgent importance, for—"

"No."

The wizard stepped back, his ominous pronouncement momentarily interrupted.

"Excuse me," he said in a slightly less stentorian tone. "But what do you mean by 'No'?"

"No means no."

"But you haven't even heard what I was going to say."

"I think I've got the gist of it. You've come to take me on some miraculous quest, probably about 1500 pages long, in which I will retrieve the sole artifact that can

127

defeat the Dark Lord and restore the world to rightful harmony. Is that more or less the story?"

The wizard looked chastened. "Well, yes, but—"

Jonathan didn't let him finish. "No buts. The answer's no."

The wizard didn't seem to know quite what to do with that. "You are the chosen one, he who is foretold by prophecy to come to the Fair Lands, fill the Crystal Chalice with the Tears of the Moon, and rally the good folk of Winterwhen to repel the forces of the *Evil One*."

Jonathan noted how the wizard managed to speak the phrase "evil one" in italics. Neat trick. He'd have to learn it if he ever took up wizarding, but not today. "I think you're going to have to find another chosen one."

"There is no other. That's sort of the point of the chosen one. Only you can find the chalice and collect the Tears of the Moon. So it is foretold."

"This prophecy mentions me by name, does it? Jonathan Harris, 35 Eastern Pkwy, Apartment 4B, Brooklyn, New York, social security number 333-78-2231?"

The wizard fingered his staff nervously. "Well, no, not in so many words, but the signs and portents all point to this time and place."

Jonathan snorted. "Prophecies aren't worth the paper they're printed on, or has your world not invented paper yet? No, don't answer that. All 'In the year of the Goat there will come a savior who knows not his power' and 'at the place where learning and nature meet' and other fribble-frabble that can mean just about anyone when you squint hard enough and look at it sideways. Not one single word that clearly and unambiguously says 'Go here. Do this.' And when the quest is complete, and the 'evil one'"—he tried to say it in italics like the wizard did, but only managed a weak pair of air quotes—"is defeated, then we'll realize that the prophecy didn't refer to me at all, but rather to my dog, or my companion, or my son, or some such thing. Meanwhile I'll have spent three years of my life sleeping rough, eating jerky and hard tack, and being poked, prodded, and tortured by orcs, only to finally restore power to the same feudal aristocracy that mismanaged the country in the first place. I have read *The Lord of the Rings,* you know. So no hard feelings, but I'm going to have to decline your offer." Jonathan tried to close the door, but the wizard had propped it open with his staff.

The wizard threw Jonathan a forced smile, but his nervousness was starting to show. Perhaps he was on a deadline? "Did I mention there's a princess? Quite comely she is too, with hair of golden flax and a face that would launch, well, maybe not a thousand ships, but I'm sure she could manage a rowboat or two."

"I'm gay."

The wizard crinkled his brow at this. "Gay? It is more traditional for the hero to be morose and troubled, overwhelmed by the heavy weight of destiny he carries on his shoulders; but I'm sure we can work with a happy, singing, protagonist."

"No, not that kind of gay. Homosexual." The wizard looked puzzled.

"Funny that you can speak such excellent English but miss this one word, almost as if same-sex attraction doesn't exist in your world." Jonathan reached for a synonym. "Queer? A friend of Dorothy? MSM? QUILTBAG? Any of this mean anything to you?"

The wizard shook his head. "I'm sorry, but no."

"I don't like women, OK? At least not like that. I like men."

"Aha," the wizard said. "In that case I'm sure we can find you a prince or maybe a barbarian warrior. The sword brothers of Skalano's tastes run in your direction."

"No offense to the good brothers of Skalano, who I'm sure do the best they can with their lot in life, but I rather prefer modern men who know about bathing and nightclubs and American Apparel. So, if it's all the same to you, I'm going to let this quest pass me by." Jonathan pushed harder against the door, but the wizard's staff was sturdier than it looked.

"If a princess won't sway you, perhaps a kingdom? That was supposed to go to Flerhara, who would later be revealed as the rightful heir in book 3, but I think we can work around that. Maybe give her true love and a small Duchy on the other side of the river instead. Haven't you ever wanted a castle of your very own? Moat, crenellations, secret passages, a banquet hall for entertaining visiting adventurers, the whole shebang."

"But no cable TV, coffee, central heating, blenders, or major appliances. I'm sure you don't have dishwashers yet."

The wizard perked up at this. "Yes, we have dishwashers! And cooks and scullery maids too!"

Jonathan rolled his eyes. "No, that isn't what I meant. No slur on your domestic staff, but I doubt they've achieved 21st century standards of hygiene. Frankly, I'd be surprised if I got a mattress without fleas."

The wizard's hat drooped. "A certain number of fleas are to be expected; but I'm sure you won't notice them, not with all the wenches and serving girls—"

"Excuse me, what part of 'gay' did you not understand?" The wizard looked puzzled again. Jonathan sighed. "OK, all of it. Let's just say that wenches and serving girls are not exactly a selling feature for me, all right? I'd much rather live here in my air conditioned, one-room apartment with 800 channels including A&E and an unlimited supply of Internet porn. Now if that's all you have, I really do have to get ready for work."

Jonathan kicked the wizard's staff out from the door. The wizard, startled, took a step backwards, which was all the space Jonathan needed. He slammed the door shut and threw the deadbolt before the old gray-hair could contrive some other reason he should leave his comfortable Brooklyn life behind to run around some medieval backwater.

Jonathan wondered if the deadbolt would be enough or if he should barricade the door against some magical attempt to shanghai him. He didn't relax until he heard the wizard's staff banging at the door of Apartment 4C.

"Roxana Jackson, I have come to fetch you on a quest of most urgent importance, for the Fair Lands are in dire peril, and only you can save them." Jonathan waited until he heard a loud pop. Then he went back to the shower.

About the Author

Elliotte Rusty Harold is originally from New Orleans, to which he returns periodically in search of a decent bowl of gumbo. However, he currently resides in the Prospect Heights neighborhood of Brooklyn with his wife Beth and dog Thor. He is the author of numerous books about software development, most recently the JavaMail API from O'Reilly.

*****~~~~~*****

Abbreviated Epics

The Blue Cup

by Marissa James

There were days when Joyce could almost see Radiance again.

The "almost" being operative, as there was no way back. After twenty-five years of yearning, she knew it for a heart-tearing certainty.

It was twenty-five years since she'd last seen the Lords of Dendarra, the Eyries of Vel, the vast emerald seas of the Numatism Isles. The lion riders and buccaneers and spice prophets and cloud maidens, the stars coming down on special nights to dance for her. The aching beauty of a place that surely must exist, because how could there be a word like beauty without Radiance?

And how could a person realize the fullness of that word, beauty, without having experienced both worlds? Water ran into the sink, submerging crusted dishes, and she added a healthy dose of double-strength cleaner. It didn't really matter how much, did it? "Lemon-scented!," the bottle said, and "Fast Acting!" and "Warning: Toxic!"

When she dozed off under a tree in her family's backyard and woke beneath a date palm in the Sha'ar Desert, she thought it was a dream, and hardly gathered her senses in time to hurry after a departing caravan of mirage hunters. A golden dragon soared overhead, the beat of its wings freezing the beat of her heart even as it caused a shower of coins. The caravaneers sheltered under the remains of a petrified forest, toppled and smoothed by centuries, as she stood transfixed by the glittering fall, diamonds and blood gems catching and twisting the sunlight into a dance of prismatic rainbow flashes.

With mere heartbeats to spare, a fleet-footed youth had snatched her hand and pulled her beneath a stony mushroom, where they huddled and watched the golden shower thunder upon the desert floor. As soon as it ended the caravaneers emerged, gathering treasure like desert plants seeking rain one drop at a time.

This encounter with Rahel the Light-Handed began the truest friendship of her life. He gave her a delicate blue cup he'd snatched from the air in the midst of saving her, and she understood why he was called that.

When she dipped the cup into a stagnant pool to clean it, the water it held became pure and sweet and fragrant, like honeyed lavender. Caravaneers claimed to see secrets in the swirling patterns on the cup's surface, and to unravel them she sought out sages and mages and apothecaries and priestesses in the City of Coral Walls. But, finally, it was an ancient, half-blind servant in the house of the second-ranked skywatcher who told her it had come from the floating city of Dendarra, a mythic place even in Radiance. Because it was her cup, it was her duty to return it to the city that, it was said, shone more beautiful than any place in Radiance Below. And Rahel tightened his gun belt and doffed his hat and declared that he would help her find the city in the air.

She unearthed a plate from the submerged dish-heap and scrubbed at its toad-green surface. She'd had the blue cup in mind when she requested this style as a wedding gift, though it had always been a stretch to see one in the other. There was nothing in this world that compared to Radiance. The very earth and air there had shined; after all, how else had Radiance earned its name? Scraping gummy white sauce from the plate, she tried to recall that shine but failed. Even when she dreamed of Radiance these days, she knew it was a dream, because nothing shined like it should.

Joyce and Rahel made Dendarra their special quest, the adventure around which their friendship evolved. If they had to walk Radiance three times over, they would find the floating land and a way to reach it. More than once a mysterious shape that wasn't dragon or roc or windcutter drifted across the sky, high and distant, sending her heart racing with hope.

Lost in the labyrinthine Nesek Steppes, they pledged the bond of blood-friends, while hyenas cackled on the breeze and the full second moon spotlighted them, Rahel with only two bullets left to protect them. They'd survived with many shared tears, whispering promises to the Lady of Shadows and one another, fingers interlaced like puzzle pieces.

In the next room a recliner creaked, and Greg whooped at the TV; some sport was going on, and some team he cared about was winning. Or perhaps the others were losing. It didn't have to be the same thing for Greg.

Greg wasn't like Rahel in any way, and it was with this acute awareness that she'd married him. It wouldn't be fair to compare her husband to someone as loyal and generous and brave as Rahel. He couldn't compare, and knowing so was comparison enough. It wasn't his fault that he'd never had the chance to do something heroic for her, any more than it was his fault her heart was like the once-flowering Worldbloom and had already unfurled itself for Rahel.

They hadn't been lovers, though; they were too young to think of each other that way at first, and, as time went on, their bond was too tight to be anything but perfect friendship. Of course they'd gained friends and fellow travelers over the years—the Dancing Twins, Dire Wolf, Khaffan, Jela and Manqui and Leeshin the Snakesinger—who'd teased about their easy smiles and need to speak only half a conversation to understand one another. When she'd lost Rahel over the third Mist Cliff, no one and nothing could console her, and she slept with one hand curling the blue cup close against her heart. Months later he managed to rejoin their party in Greyfall, miraculously alive and whole and accompanied by the beautifully graceful Ina the Hawk. She'd cried upon seeing them, healthy and normal and happy, but hadn't been able to say why. Not then, at least.

She scrubbed hard at a bowl, wiping her sniffling nose on the back of a hand. It was the chemical cleaner biting into her sensitive nostrils. She'd put in too much, maybe.

Of course it wasn't the cleaner. It was the bronze forests of Turendal, the Flute Towers of the Bleak Waste that sang the mournful chronicles of lost civilizations with every passing wind. It was the fact that Rahel—and everyone in Radiance, for that matter—pronounced her name "Joyous."

It was the fact that she had been.

They'd sailed the Midnight Sea on a ship made of glass with a captain made of gears, and halfway across, the ship had shattered in a spellstorm. The shimmering decks dissolved into sand, and the captain and his automata crew fell limp and lifeless beneath the waves. Hand in hand, she and Rahel and the Twins and Ina swam to the end of their senses.

She awoke in a strange place of living architecture, where everything down to the sills of the windows and posts of her bed looped and curled and twined, arabesques dancing an entrancing slow-motion ballet that were all parts of the same creature or entity that was, in actuality, the city of Dendarra.

That was when she met the First Lord of Dendarra, entering her room on limbs long and graceful and tawny as a gazelle's, eyes and hair obsidian black. In his hands he bore a blue cup—her blue cup—brimming with nectar sweeter-smelling than anything she knew. He brought it to her side, put the cup in her hands, and said,

"Drink."

She did, and learned the sweetness of Dendarran lunar wine, made from the purest night dew and sweetened further by the enchantment of the cup. With one taste, her mind came brightly alive, her whole body

136

scintillating with the same shine that rose up from the earth of Radiance; she became a part of Radiance, and Radiance a part of her, a part that had been inside her since first coming to this land but that, now, she was free to see fully. When she joined her friends after that drink they shone with the same inner beauty, and Rahel like the third moon rising in a summer dawn.

All of it from that humble blue cup and sweet, sweet lunar wine.

Hands sudsed and clinging with bits of limp salad, she elbowed at her blurring eyes. The memory of that perfect sweetness always brought loss bubbling in her stomach, a harsh acid that bit until tears and sorrow welled up. Greg already thought she was in desperate need of a psych evaluation or at least a pill that would stop the breakdowns that were becoming more frequent; in truth, this meant that the memories were becoming more real and lucid than the gray soulless world around her. More than once she caught herself having conversations with Rahel or other friends she'd left behind all those years ago. Greg shook his head whenever he caught those memory-laden tears shining in her eyes, whenever she hummed tunes he didn't know or mumbled in languages that didn't exist.

After discovering Dendarra, what had there been? Ah, yes—the twins found work as acrobats and musicians, dancers and jesters. Ina so impressed the Lords of Dendarra that they gave her the gloriously arduous task of sky-patroller for the floating city. Joyce discovered that the curving shapes on the outside of her cup were part of a story, the remainder of which was scribed onto other sacred objects of Dendarra. With the help of the First Lord's son she set about translating it and piecing together the whole story—a greater task than either of them could have believed.

Only after weeks, perhaps months, of such arduous work did she realize a change. She saw her friends infrequently, and rarely gave them the attention they deserved, as her mind unraveled declensions and tenses and conjunctions instead. When she sought out Rahel to apologize, she found him on a balcony watching the dance of the cloud maidens. And somewhere between the last time she'd seen him—really, actually seen him—and this time, he'd changed. Grown taller? Older? Was it the fact that he no longer wore his broad brimmed hat because of the winds that swept the city, the fact that he'd stored away the gun belt that used to ride crooked on his hips, had traded his rough cockatrice-leather boots for soft shoes? They talked, but there was a distance between the words she said and what he heard; she saw it in his face.

It could have stayed the same between them, never changed, if only they had always had the adventure. If they'd always had Dendarra in their future, always that shimmering, impossible hope to make them gaze breathless into the softly clouded sky. There was no longer adventure in her future, so looking back occupied her time, not only in the unearthing of archives and translations. Seeing how things had changed with Rahel recalled to mind her family in the ordinary world, left behind how long ago? What changes had her absence brought to their lives?

In the shimmering aurora dawn she told him. She was going back. Being a loyal friend he'd said yes. Even if he would never see her again, she ought to do what felt right, for they would always be friends under the triple moons of Radiance. Even if this was only the sort of lie one friend was obliged to say to another.

As soon as he finished saying it, she saw the distance between them as a physical thing—love, or the uncultivated beginnings of love. If tended properly it could have grown into a thing as magnificent as the living city all around them.

One last dish; she shook it dry, toweled it off, placed it in the rack.

She'd refused thoughts of love, like thoughts of home, for all of her time in Radiance. And finally, when she faced them, it was too late.

She pulled the sink plug, watched murky water swirl down.

If she'd been wiser she would have stayed. Would have understood love for what it was: the next adventure Radiance had to offer.

After so many years without Radiance, it was a wonder she could still remember the sound of the sea wolves' howl, the Twins' laughter, the glow-in-the-day brightness of Ina the Hawk's eyes and the softness of her velvet wings. The shimmering air and indescribable beauty and Rahel's calloused hands pulling her to safety even as they plucked a blue cup out of the sky and offered it as a promise of eternal friendship.

The water drained away to nothing, and Joyce blinked in surprise; there, in the corner of her sink, the very same blue cup that had no equal in Radiance Below and certainly not in this world. Perhaps she was dreaming; but, it hadn't been a dream the first time, twenty-five years ago. She was only distantly aware of the greasy bubbles and choking chemical smell of the water slopping over the rim as she raised the cup in a shaky hand. But there was also the faint fragrance of honeyed lavender promising that the cup's purifying magic was at work even in this realm. If she would ever have a second chance at forever this was it.

She raised the cup to her lips. Even before she tasted it her mouth filled with the sweet sweet glow of Radiance.

###

About the Author

When not inhabiting a variety of fantastic worlds, Marissa James lives, works, and studies in Portland, Oregon. Her interests include obscure archaeology, peculiar books, eclectic music, and her husband, who is quick to remind her of his inimitable, muse-like properties. Her short fiction has been published by Crossed Genres, Daily Science Fiction, and Third Flatiron, among others, and will also be forthcoming in the *Torn Pages* anthology from Weird Bard Press. You can also visit her at www.marissajames.blogspot.com, where she wouldn't mind at all for you to say hello.

*****~~~~~*****

Toward the Back

by Jake Teeny

Ahead of them, the final battle for the soul of the world raged; fate decided by the edge of a blade, not the dice of the gods. Thousands of orcs, clad in shambles of black metal, wielding mangled and cockeyed blades, tramped down the hill to confront their human adversaries. The hot summer air was chalky with dust and filled with war cries, clanging weapons, and the last breaths of those sprawled across the yellowy fields.

"The humans have a great color scheme, though, don't they?" said the orc infantryman Globbergarg, or Glob as his friends called him.

"To be honest," replied Mardar'carnik, or Teacup as his friends called him, "I think it's a little garish. The red and silver tries too hard to convey, 'humanity will prevail!' I've always liked black and gold."

"Oh, yes. Black and gold are nice."

Glob and Teacup stood toward the back of their battalion. Ahead, the swarm of fellow soldiers began to slow, the frontlines of man and orc finally clashing with quaking violence.

"Didn't we see that somewhere before?" asked Glob. With winged ears, lumpy gray skin, and a snout seemingly sheared from a pig's, Glob was a good-looking orc.

"See what?"

"That black and gold color scheme."

"Was it the Renwalls?"

"No, they had those brown and blue tunics with the—"

"With the big fish on the front." Teacup shuddered. "Terrible."

"So terrible. Who wants their sigil to be a fish?"

"Can you imagine the conversation their founders must have had?" Teacup squalled his voice to mimic the humans. "'What animal should we choose as our insignia? A bear? No, too vicious. How about a wolf? No, too awesome. Oh, I've got it! A fish! You know, the only animal that is eaten by *every other animal in the world.*'"

Glob laughed. "Stupid humans."

"It's like they want to be conquered," continued Teacup. "If you can't even decide on—"

"Hey!" barked an orc to their left, the commander of this tail battalion, Riser Har'n'Zerk. Two heads taller than the rest of the grunts, he had solid black eyes and twin heaving slits for a nose. "What's going on here?"

Glob glanced at Teacup. "Just screaming and pounding our weapons, sir."

"That's right," said Teacup. "Just promoting the promulgation of evilness, sir."

Riser Har'n'Zerk glared at them. "I'm watching you. . . The Shadowed One does not tolerate disobedience."

"We are all about obedience, sir," said Teacup.

"Yes," added Glob. "May the deeds of His Shadowyness forever continue in darkness and displeasure."

"Amen."

"Amen."

Riser Har'n'Zerk towered over them just a moment longer. "You better be boasting the warrior's paint when I return," threatened their battalion commander. "Glob. Teamug. Don't disappoint me." Riser Har'n'Zerk turned and pushed his way back through the throng of orcs.

"It's Tea*cup*, you buffoon," muttered Teacup.

"What's the difference?"

"What do you mean?"

"I mean, what's the difference between a Teacup and a Teamug?"

Teacup stared blankly at his friend. "Tea*mugs* don't exist."

"No need to get snappy."

"I'm not getting snappy."

"You had a tone."

"We're at war. I'm entitled a tone."

"Not toward me you aren't."

Teacup huffed and shook his head. "You don't understand. Your nickname. . . '

"Glob? It's just the shortened version of Globbergarg. It's—" The line of orcs behind them pushed forward, and the two were nearly shoved to the dirt. Abiding their comrades' wishes, Glob and Teacup stormed forward, before another line of stalled orcs halted them.

"Now, what were you saying?" asked Glob, once each of them had straightened the metal scraps hung over their bodies.

"Oh, never mind," sighed Teacup. "Look at the view." Atop the crest of the hill, the whole battle, the horde of orcs on one side, the allegiance of humans on the other, warred with ringing swords and the rush of arrows.

"See, now an archer would be an all right job," said Glob.

"Stand in the back, fire into the masses. Safety. Distance. I get you."

"Hey," said Glob, his stomach gurgling, "you don't happen to have any extra food, do you?"

"I told you to eat a big breakfast this morning."

"I wasn't hungry this morning."

"Neither was I," said Teacup, reaching behind to pluck the string of his loincloth from burying deeper. "And that squirrel fricassee the slaves made was awful."

"*Awful!*"

"Burnt and stringy. You'd think they never cooked by campfire before."

"I thought some rosemary would have added some needed flavor."

"Rosemary would have been perfect," said Teacup.

"Try convincing Riser Har'n'*Jerk* that rosemary is a necessary expenditure, though."

"Clever. Har'n'Jerk. You come up with that?"

"I'll be honest. I overheard Flea Gut use it," said Glob.

"What happened to Flea Gut? I haven't seen him in a while."

"Got pitted on a lance, and now the humans parade his head around before battles."

"He was an ugly orc," said Teacup.

"God, I never wanted to say it, but wasn't he? His eyes. . . "

"Hideous."

"I swear they were so far to the side of his head he could see inside his ears."

"Not that he'd want to look in there. He had terrible hygiene."

"Terrible," agreed Glob.

A commotion drew their attention to the left, where they found Riser Har'n'Zerk to be marching toward them again.

"The paint!" said Glob.

"Get the human blood from your pouch," hissed Teacup.

Glob hesitated. "I can't."

"What do you mean you can't?"

"I told you I was hungry…"

Teacup scowled. "I had to chip that off of three orcs' armor, and then stir it with water for ten minutes before I got the proper consistency!"

"I asked you if you had any food. . . "

"You know he's going to send us to the front lines to get more," hissed Teacup.

"Quick! Grab some mud."

"What?" But Glob had already bent over and begun to smear mud across his face. Cursing, Teacup did the same, standing just as Riser Har'n'Zerk loomed before them.

"What's this?" growled the commander.

Both Teacup and Glob feigned confusion and looked around. "Were you speaking to us?" asked Glob.

"Of course!" roared Riser Har'n'Zerk. "What's that on your face?"

"This?" said Teacup. "Just your typical, standard issued, human blood, sir."

"Yes," said Glob. "The blood of our forsworn and eternal enemy. Let the True Shadow stretch on forever!"

A cry from nearby orcs echoed the sentiment. "Nice one," whispered Teacup.

"Human blood? Why's it so thick? And brown?"

"Very good question, sir, ' said Glob. "Teacup?"

"Well, you see," began Teacup, giving Glob a sidelong glance, "with the angle of the sun in conjunction with the dilution of our perspiration—"

"Enough!" growled their commander. "Just make sure you add a fresh coat when you reach the frontlines."

"Of course, sir," said Glob.

"Indubitably," said Teacup.

Satisfied, Riser Har'n'Zerk tramped through the other orcs and back to his center position.

"Does he have a thing for us or something?" said Glob, exhaling with relief.

"Thanks for putting me on the spot there."

"You did great. Conjunction. Dilution. I knew you'd come up with some big words to confuse him."

Teacup looked down, abashed. "It's not all about who can swing their sword the fastest."

Another push came from the orcs behind them, and both Teacup and Glob were elbowed forward. Unlike last time, however, they covered close to thirty strides, the front lines of the battle now less than the length of a mighty warship.

"We're getting close, aren't we," said Glob. "Makes you, uh, makes you hunger for human flesh, doesn't it?"

"Yeah," said Teacup, swallowing with a dry throat. "Makes you, uh, want to stab things."

"Human things."

"Yeah—Whoa! Did you see that?" Ahead of them a hundred strides, a swirl of steel slashed and felled orcs like a bladed tornado.

"Is that. . . Is that. . . "

"*Laytannon*."

"The Gods' Hilt."

Both Teacup and Glob stared in wonder at the man, the pinnacle of human fighters. Infamous for his golden haired ponytail and water-like elusiveness, every orc knew his name. And every orc knew to fear him.

"Well," said Teacup, "that's not good." Behind him, other oinking orcs jostled them forward.

"I heard that after battle, he eats all the hearts of those he's slain," said Glob.

"That's just myth," said Teacup, his sword loose in his sweaty palms.

"I also heard that an orc once cut off his hand, but it just grew right back."

"Impossible," gulped Teacup.

"I even heard—"

"None of that's real," said Teacup, though not as resolutely as he would have liked. "In fact, you know what I heard? I heard that woman-humans say he has a tiny genital."

Glob puzzled his face. "Where'd you hear that?"

"From some orcs." Teacup shrugged.

Glob pondered a moment. "I guess on the battlefield, though, that doesn't really help us, does it?"

"No," said Teacup. "That doesn't really help us at all."

Again, a gap formed ahead of them, and Glob and Teacup were forced to dash forward. When they stopped, humans and orcs fought less than twenty strides away.

"You know what I was thinking?" asked Glob, as he shifted to allow the more inspired orcs to pass him and enter the melee.

"What's that, Glob?"

"I was thinking I didn't properly clean my spare sword back at camp. And a rusty sword is a useless sword."

"Very useless."

"So I'm thinking. . . maybe I go back there and clean it real fast?"

"And I'll go with you," offered Teacup. "Just to make sure I cleaned my spare as well."

"That's a good idea." Glob glanced at the shouting orcs around him. "So, should we. . ."

"Maybe bend down and pretend like we have to pick a rock from our toes?" said Teacup. "Then just kind of. . . crouch, crawl back to camp?"

"I'm good with crouching and crawling."

Both orcs slowly lowered themselves to the ground, when suddenly a hand on the back of each orc's head yanked them up.

"What's this!" bellowed Riser Har'n'Zerk.

"Right in my ear," muttered Glob, rubbing a finger in it.

"We were just doing some stretches, sir," said Teacup. "Didn't want to pull a—"

"Why are you just standing here?" roared the commander. "Into battle!"

"Just prepping, sir," said Glob.

"That's right," said Teacup. "Calisthenics make the body a more reactive weapon."

"Now! Fight!" Riser Har'n'Zerk shoved both orcs forward. Open ground formed around them, and from directly ahead, a human solder with a sword already buried in his shoulder, ran deliriously toward them.

"Sword hand up, step, swing, pivot," muttered Glob as the human approached, but at the last moment, Glob closed his eyes and just waited for the impact of the other man's weapon. Instead, however, the thunk came outside of Glob's body, and when he looked, Teacup had rammed his sword into the man's head.

"Did you see that?" said Teacup. "Did you see me just—Boom. Bam. Woosh!" Teacup reenacted the chopping motion with his arm.

"You just. . . You just. . . " Glob's eyes gleamed with tears. "Thank you, Teacup. You just saved my life."

Teacup shrugged nonchalantly and made to retrieve his blade. "Killing's in my blood. My father trained me when—" Teacup struggled to remove his sword from the other man's skull. "Wow. I really jammed it in there." He put a foot on the limp body and yanked back with all his strength. With a gush, the blade came free, splattering both orcs with mushy brain and blood.

"Disgusting," cried Glob, wiping a hand down his face.

Stumbling, Teacup apologized and spit out some of the flung flesh. "Well, we got that second coat Commander told us to get."

"I guess you're right," said Glob. Each orc hesitated a moment. "So. . . back to clean our spare blades?"

"Yes. I think so." But when they turned around, they saw that Riser Har'n'Zerk stood not ten paces away fighting off three humans.

"Do you think he sees us?" asked Glob.

"I don't know," said Teacup. "Let's just—" He looked around, finding orcs engaged in battle on all sides. "Let's just keep stabbing this human."

"The one you just killed?"

"No one'll know. And once Riser Har'n'Jerk leaves—"

"Or dies."

"—or, yes, preferably dies, we'll head back to camp."

"Good plan," said Glob, beginning to hack at the corpse on the ground. "One problem, though. . . " He glanced around them. "I've kind of got to go to the bathroom."

"I told you to go this morning," said Teacup, adding a couple whacks to the human's legs.

"I did go this morning. An orc can go more than once a day, you know."

"So just pull up your loincloth and go. I won't look."

"But we're surrounded," said Glob. "I won't be able to go with everyone looking at me."

"No one's looking at you." The human body at their feet made a gurgling noise, followed by the release of a noxious odor. "See? He just went."

Glob scowled. "Seriously, Teacup, I don't know how much longer I can hold it."

"Just kind of. . . go while you're standing there, then."

"Down my leg?"

"I don't know! Besides, we have a larger problem. This body, here, is clearly looking a little too dead." The human before them had become a flayed slop of red flesh and cracked bones.

"Hey, Teacup. . . Teacup. . . "

"I mean, maybe if we reattached the head or something."

"Hey, Teacup. Look."

Following his fellow orc's advice, Teacup looked.

Directly ahead of them, dressed in resplendent plate armor, an ornamental sword hilt painted on his chest, approached Laytannon.

Teacup puffed his cheeks out and held his breath a moment. "Well, that is some seriously bad luck."

The God's Hilt weaved toward them, his mighty bastard sword dripping with lavender blood, the attacks of fellow orcs like dry leaves trying to break through a brick wall.

"Ideas," said Teacup. "This would be a very good time for ideas."

"Hey, Teacup," said Glob. "I solved my bathroom issue."

"I figured you would."

With one swipe of his sword, Laytannon beheaded three orcs, before he turned to parry another blow and plunge his blade into an orc's sternum.

"My initial thought," said Teacup, "and work with me on this one, is to drop our swords and run in the complete opposite direction."

"Sounds good so far."

"Anything to add?"

"Maybe push down a couple orcs as we run? Slow him down a little?"

"Good. Good," said Teacup, nodding. "And if we see—"

Just then, Laytannon stepped into the clearing four strides from Teacup and Glob. His brown eyes were even more deadly and beautiful close up, his golden hair, sweaty and unraveled, just as stunning as the stories claimed. When his eyes fell to the mangled body at the two orcs' feet, however, an invisible blow appeared to strike Laytannon.

"Little Baydin. . . " he whispered. Suddenly, The Gods' Hilt looked up, anger like molten steel filling his eyes. "You killed my nephew! You killed Little Baydin!"

Teacup and Glob both pursed their lips and looked at one another. "Us?" asked Glob.

"No, no," said Teacup. "That was Thar'rog over there."

"Yes," said Glob. "All Thar'rog. We actually tried to stop him."

"That we did, didn't we, Glob?"

"Sure did, Teacup. Thar'rog's the one with the nose ring and scar beneath—"

"The gods hear me," cried Laytannon. "I will have my vengeance in blood and bone!"

"Actually," said Teacup, hurriedly reaching into a side pouch, "how about having your vengeance in squirrel jerky? It's full of nutrients and gives something to chew on for hours."

"You had food this whole time?" hissed Glob.

"Why should I be forced to share, when I thought ahead?"

The Gods' Hilt roared. "Now! Both of you! Prepare to die!"

"You should really understand, though," said Glob, "Teacup was the one who killed your nephew."

"What?"

"I just kind of closed my eyes and held my hands up. I didn't even see it."

Teacup dropped his sword and raised his hands. "Yeah, but Glob helped mutilate the body. He was the one who cut off the head."

Glob, too, dropped his sword and raised his hands. "But, I mean, c'mon, he was already dead by then. No point bemoaning spilled deer's blood."

"That saying isn't even applicable, here," blurted Teacup.

Without warning, Laytannon leapt forward, his sword arced high above his head. But as he brought it down on the closed-eyed, quivering Glob and Teacup, a sharp ring of metal staved the blade.

Riser Har'n'Zerk deflected the strike.

With a barbaric roar, the commander pushed back Laytannon's blade and swung at his human foe. Just as thunderously, Laytannon swung back, and a dance of metal and muscles ensued.

"Take his flank!" roared the Riser over the clang of metal.

"The flank?" asked Glob.

"The backside."

"Oh." Glob bit his lower lip. "I don't really see that happening."

"Me neither."

"So what, we just stand here and watch?"

"Maybe pick up our swords first?" suggested Teacup. Both orcs bent to retrieve their weapons.

"And will you look at this," complained Glob. "I've got mud all over my blade."

"Me, too," said Teacup. "How unfortunate."

"You know what this means."

Teacup sighed disappointedly. "Looks like we have to head back to camp."

"Back to camp," echoed Glob.

"I mean, that's where all the best cleaning supplies are."

"How come you remembered to pack extra food but no rags and lather?"

"Silly mistake."

"Very silly."

The commander again roared at them to assist in battling Laytannon, but Teacup and Glob just uttered apologies.

"We'll be right back," said Glob.

"Right back," said Teacup.

"We'll clean these blades, do a little stretching—"

"Get you some food."

"—get me some food, then we'll be right back to help you."

"You need anything from camp?" asked Teacup.

Just grunts and clattering metal came as response.

152

Toward the Back

"Okay, never mind, then," said Teacup, he and Glob turning around to slip between the orcs charging the opposite direction.

"You think, maybe we should. . . "

"Fake an injury?" suggested Teacup.

"Brilliant," said Glob.

Together, each orc with his sword arm pressed against his chest and his head hung low, limped back toward camp.

###

About the Author

Jake Teeny graduated from Santa Clara University with a dual degree in philosophy and psychology and now attends Ohio State University for a doctorate in social psychology. When not conducting research, he loves to write fiction, play basketball, and list items in groups of threes. A catalog of his published work as well as his weekly blog, "Psychophilosophy Tips for Everyday Living" can be found at www.JakeTeeny.com

*****~~~~~*****

The Lost Children

by Alison McBain

When the midwives came running out the door, crying, Minos rushed into the birthing room. His wife already had the two babies at her breast. The one on the left waved her hands gently as she nursed, but did not turn her head to look up at him. Her long-lashed eyes were closed against the brown hair covering her face, her bovine lips suckling intently. The one on the right kicked his hooves, blinking his sleepy human eyes at the king standing frozen in the doorway. Minos stared at Pasiphaë with horror.

"They are born from your arrogance," his wife told him wearily. There was a note of triumph in her voice. "You would not honor Poseidon by sacrificing the white bull. And I have fallen in love with the bull as deeply as you have."

Minos looked at the two half-creatures, part human and part calf. "More deeply, it would seem," he said. Dazed, he slowly started to walk towards her. "I will kill these monsters. And you," he added belatedly. "For making a fool of me and sinning with the god's beast."

"The bull was Poseidon's gift to you, but you would not sacrifice him as the god commanded. If you had killed him when you were supposed to, this would never have happened. The goddess Aphrodite has already come to bless these children. Would you argue with the gods?"

"I have before," said Minos. He was human, and he had made mistakes. He should have done what the gods had told him, and he had, as his wife said, been arrogant. He shrank back against the wall, feeling suddenly old and spent of his fury. "Very well. But expect nothing more from me except for your lives."

Pasiphaë raised her chin. "I have never expected more. And you have given to me the nothing you promised, over and over again."

...

By the king's decree, the children were allowed to live, and indeed, their lives were peaceful. They stayed in Pasiphaë's rooms at first. The girl, Agaphya, was a gentle and docile daughter. She did exactly what she was told, but couldn't manipulate her large cow's tongue to speak human language, and so remained mute. Her brother, Asterion, grew at an alarming rate, the same as any bull. Within half a year, it was hard for him to enter through the narrow doorway leading to his mother's room. Within a year, he was forced to spend his days outside, in a covered tent rigged up for him in the courtyard with the assistance of his mother's handmaids. Although his body grew at a bull's rate, his head grew at a human's rate, so he had the small baby face of a one-year-old perched atop his strong bull's neck.

Agaphya refused to be separated from her brother. If she was taken away for even so much as a moment, she would wobble her large cow's head atop her small baby's neck and low and low endlessly. The sound was inescapable, her moaning cow cries impossible to hush. Finally, their mother allowed the girl to toddle out to her brother and sleep against his warm side at night. The girl spent her days riding on Asterion as he walked around the courtyard, her legs split wide over the expanse of his broad back. He was careful of his hooves around the tiny girl when she walked on her own feet, and one could tell where his sister was standing simply by the direction in which he pointed his face at any given time. They were like one creature separated into two bodies—or, more correctly, two creatures meant to be one.

The king's subjects grew so used to having these two as a fixture at the palace that it sometimes came as a shock when visiting dignitaries expressed fear or disgust at seeing them for the first time. The only one who never seemed to accept them was Minos, who took pains to avoid the main courtyard. When he was forced to cross it, he would hurry by and never look up at the two children-beasts there. And they would watch him silently, never speaking or drawing attention to themselves. Their mother had told them about Minos. What she had said was best left unrepeated.

Twelve years passed, and Asterion's face lengthened, grew larger and more proportionate with his bull's body. Agaphya's huge cow head no longer tended to overtip her if she walked too quickly, for she grew taller and broader. By age sixteen, the two halves of their nature seemed to settle into a complementary whole, a blending together of things as intended by the gods.

But the more content the two siblings seemed, the more the king's face grew wrathful every time he happened to spot them. When he overheard his counselors speaking about these two creatures as "The Minotaurs," some sort of benevolent symbol for the city, he was furious. This was *his* city, not a place for the foul offspring of his wife's adultery. He needed to do something, and that something came about through listening to his wife, incidentally enough.

He hadn't touched Pasiphaë since the birth. Not brushed a sleeve past hers or put a hand on her skin. He had barely seen her. But at important state functions, he needed a queen as hostess for the appearance of things, and so several times a year, he would summon her to attend court. She always came and fulfilled her duties impeccably. But the slow burn of hatred in his heart engendered by her deceitful presence took weeks to disperse again.

This time was no exception. Even though he had summoned her, upon seeing Pasiphaë's still-beautiful face, Minos was overwhelmed for a moment with rage. He had to take several deep breaths before he could speak. "We have visitors from the mainland," he told her.

"Very well."

"I will send you the details via your handmaiden. Tomorrow is the feast. I want you to show them all honors."

"Of course. Is there anything else?"

The presumption of the woman! He seethed, but finally shook his head. He did not trust his voice. She turned and left without saying anything else, without once meeting his eyes.

The next night, with the envoys of kings at his side, he couldn't help but hear the words of his wife as she conversed with one of the ambassadors two seats away. "I would never dare!" she laughed—flirtatiously, he thought.

"It is not as scary as it is made out to be," grinned the man. He toyed with the grapes on his plate, as if giving his hands something to do while his attention was diverted by a beautiful woman. "In fact, it was over quite quickly."

"I have always wondered about the oracle." Pasiphaë's voice lowered, and Minos couldn't hear what was said next.

"Yes, I know. I saw them as I came in," replied the ambassador.

That very night, Minos commanded his ships be readied for sailing in the morning. If that man could find answers at Delphi's oracle, so could he. He was a king, after all. And the gods bent special favor upon his kind.

…

When he returned, Minos brought shiploads of new people with him, crowds of architects and slaves. They set to work immediately. The oracle had told him to build a maze underneath his palace, a massive cage for the two unnatural godspawn creatures. Once that was done, he was to leave them trapped in the center.

158

Work proceeded quickly. He was unsurprised to see Pasiphaë when she eventually came to visit him, her face as pale as cheese.

"You can't mean to do this. They are *children*."

"They are monsters," he told her coldly. "I should have done this long before."

She pleaded, she begged for their lives. He relented enough that a small chute was built in the center of the palace, so food and drink could be dropped down for those below. "This is your responsibility," he told her. "I will have no one help you in this task. You must prepare the food with your own hands and bring it to them. If you fail in that, I will have rocks thrown down instead, and the entrance sealed."

The queen bowed her head. "Thank you for your generosity, King Minos." She could not quite contain the bitterness in her tone.

"Be careful, wife," he told her. "Lest I force their adulterous mother to join them. Then there would be no one left to feed you."

Pasiphaë bowed her head lower. This time, she did not trust her voice to speak. At her apparent humility, he let her take leave of his presence.

…

When her children were blindfolded, twenty strong men had to restrain Asterion as he used every bit of his bull's strength to try and escape. Agaphya, docile as always, meekly allowed her head to be covered with a sack and followed the hands that guided her. Pasiphaë wept as her children were led into the labyrinth, but made no move to stop the soldiers who took them. She knew King Minos's eyes were on her. She knew, but did not care, except to fervently remind herself that her children would die without her. She needed to stay strong of heart.

Each day before the sun rose, Pasiphaë trekked down to the marketplace and purchased the freshest foodstuffs she could find. Then back to the palace kitchens, where she would spend hours chopping and stirring, creating simple but nutritious fare. She would tie the meals up in a cloth and lower them on a string through the palace chute. When she felt the tug on the other end, she counted a double handful of numbers, and then brought the string back up, with only the cloth at the end of it, now emptied of viands.

After a year passed, King Minos summoned her again. "There is a delegation from Athens," he told her. "They have spoken to the oracle."

"What now?" she asked warily.

"Plague," he replied. "The oracle told them to sacrifice a boy and girl to the creatures underneath our city."

"Sacrifice? Creatures? They are no more violent than I am! They are children, still, and you have imprisoned them. What have they ever done to you?"

Minos loomed over her. "They were born," he said. "That is enough." There was nothing she could argue against that. He continued, "You must lead the sacrifices to the center of the maze."

"How am I to do that? I have never been inside the labyrinth. I don't know my way to the center."

For the first time, Minos smiled. It was not a friendly expression. "You will learn."

…

In the end, her handmaiden came up with the answer. "String," the woman said. "Tie a piece to the entrance to guide you back through any wrong turnings."

It worked like a charm. Although the boy and girl from Athens were frightened after many hours traveling through the labyrinth, and upon finally seeing the two creatures who awaited them, Pasiphaë managed to reassure them. "These two will not hurt you," she told the sacrifices. "They are my children."

The Athenian delegation, satisfied when she came back by herself, went on their way. Pasiphaë sent even more food down the chutes to care for the extra mouths. A year later, the Athenians returned.

"Plague? The oracle?" she guessed when Minos summoned her.

"Yes," he said without preamble. She led the two new children to the center of the maze and spent many hours of each day after that preparing food for the prisoners in the labyrinth. A year later, the ships returned.

This time, Minos declared that he would celebrate their arrival with a feast. The oracle had told the Athenians that this third time would permanently end the plague that had troubled them. Pasiphaë sat next to the ambassador, the young son of the Athenian king, and spoke with him throughout the long night. Afterwards, she took to her bed, exhausted from the celebrations. Tomorrow, she would lead the last of the children into the maze.

But the next morning, she was feverish and crying out at the pain. Minos, arriving to summon her to the maze, looked down at his wife and saw the telltale boils rising to the surface of her skin. Pasiphaë was insensible, unaware that he was even standing over her. "Tend to her," he told her handmaiden. "And send the ambassador to me."

The young man came immediately. Theseus, Minos recalled. "The queen has fallen to Athens' plague," he said. The young man appeared startled.

"But the oracle said. . . "

"Only one thing can cure her. An end to this dreadful disease. Bring the final sacrifices to the center of the maze. Do not come back until you have done so."

"But I do not know the way. Only the queen knows."

"Do not trouble me with useless details. Ask her, if you are so inclined."

With a sinking feeling, the prince knocked at the entrance to her rooms. The handmaiden allowed him into the queen's chambers, but Pasiphaë was tossing back and forth and couldn't answer his questions.

"I know a way," said a soft voice behind him. He turned to see the queen's handmaiden, a woman a little older than Pasiphaë. "String," she explained to him.

As he went into the labyrinth, Theseus took the children with one hand and held the string with the other. Although he made many wrong turnings through the twisting corridors of the stone maze, hours later, he made the final turning and saw a sea of light.

Or so it seemed, after such a long time in the darkness. At the center of the enormous cavern at the labyrinth's end, a small fire was burning. Four children sat around its perimeter, black with smoke and filth. They cowered back at his sudden appearance, at the rage on his face when he saw them. Here were all the sacrifices demanded by the oracle. No wonder Athens had continued to suffer plague, if all these sacrifices still lived. It was the deepest betrayal of the gods.

Suddenly, he heard a sound to his left and looked over to see two monstrous creatures approaching him. One thundered towards him like a galloping horse, and he dropped the string he was holding and reached for his sword.

When he emerged from the entrance to the labyrinth hours later, having followed the string back to its source, the soldiers at the entrance gaped at him. Theseus wiped a bloody hand across his face, but it didn't improve his appearance. One of the men at the entrance tentatively asked, "Were you successful?"

Theseus looked down at his bloody hands. "Yes," he said shortly. "They are all dead."

The man's eyes widened. "All, your Highness?"

"I have made answer to the gods' demands for sacrifice."

"Bad news, then, your Highness," said the other soldier. "The city mourns. The queen died while you were below. I am truly sorry. You must not have been in time."

Theseus smiled grimly. "The gods have spoken through me," he said. "And I *was* successful. I got there just in the nick of time."

About the Author

Alison McBain lives in Connecticut with her husband and two daughters. She has publications in Flash Fiction Online, Abyss & Apex, and On the Premises, among others. Earlier this year, she also received the Patricia McFarland Memorial Award from Flash Fiction Chronicles. You can read her blog at alisonmcbain.com or follow her on Twitter @AlisonMcBain.

*****~~~~~*****

Abbreviated Epics

Great Light's Daughters

by Patricia S. Bowne

Long ago, when the earth was new and everything was brown, Great Light went away for a while. Everything living on the earth was frightened. How could they live in darkness? They all cried out, from the smallest plant to the largest water-beast. "Great Light, do not forsake us!" they cried.

Great Light heard, and sent his eight daughters to watch over the earth. They floated high above it, and if their light was nothing compared to Great Light, it was enough to comfort most of the earth's creatures. Only the big-toothed creatures could not endure without Great Light, and this is why you find only their bones today.

Great Light's daughters were taller than the trees, and their skin was silver like the first morning light on the water-fields or the last evening light on the ocean. They had hair so long it wrapped around their feet. They sat upon the clouds and spun cloud-stuff into thread as fine as hens'-hair.

It happened one day that the eldest of Great Light's daughters dropped her spindle, all the way onto the earth.

"Nuisance!" she cried, and the creatures below felt a tremble go through the ground. "What is it trapped on?" For when she picked up the spindle, her thread had remained, tangled among the plants of earth and the jagged mountains. "Sisters, I can't get it loose."

The second sister reached down and found one piece of the thread. Her fingers dug deep into the ground on each side of it as she grasped it. That is Fountain Gorge, where the water falls so far. One day, children, you may see it. But Great Light's second daughter couldn't pull the thread loose either, and she had to let it go.

One by one, all of Great Light's daughters tried to pick up their sister's thread, but they all failed. Do you know why? Some say the spider underground had clutched it tight, and scurried with the end of it into her lair. They say she died of envy that day, as she sat in her lair handling the thread, or that she killed herself trying to spin silk that fine, and since she died there is nobody left alive who can venture that far down in the earth, to free the trapped thread of Great Light's first daughter.

"What a bother," said Great Light's first daughter. "All that work, for nothing!" She had to bite off her thread short to the spindle, gather new cloud-stuff and start again. Now she spun harder than before, to catch up to her sisters. But she was far behind.

Now, we all know that when the older sister lags behind, the younger sisters shirk. So it was with Great Light's younger daughters. They looked at their elder sister's empty spindle from the corners of their eyes, and then at one another's full spindles, and their eyes said, "We are far ahead of her," and "Why should we work so hard?" By and by, they began to get up from where they had sat spinning, and to wander over the clouds. Because clouds are not flat, children, you know; they are sometimes piled up into mountains and palaces, sometimes gold and sometimes pink or purple, or crystal blue. Great Light's younger daughters played hide-and-seek among the clouds, and the light on the earth shifted and glinted as they ran.

Great Light's youngest daughter hid so well that none of the others could find her. Waiting, she grew bored. Finally she lay down and put her face through the clouds to watch what was happening on the earth, and what do you think she saw? Right across the earth, where her sister's thread had fallen, was a green line of trees, growing so high they almost touched the clouds. Birds of every color bustled among them, monkeys and unicorns, dragonets and bright butterflies. It was the most exciting thing Great Light's youngest daughter had ever seen, because there are no bright colors up in Great Light's house. "How wonderful!" she cried, reaching down from her cloud. She gathered up colors, one after another, purple and coral and scarlet, and spun them into her thread. Just then she heard her sisters calling, growing closer; so she hid her spindle in a hollow of the cloud and ran out for her sisters to find her, and they played for the rest of the day.

That evening, Great Light's youngest daughter did not have her spindle. She ran back to the cloud for it, but clouds are changeable things, and the one she had left her spindle in was gone! Do you know where it went, children? When you see the rainbow, you see youngest daughter's spindle with the colored thread trailing behind it.

Youngest daughter began to cry when she found her spindle gone. "I will never catch up with the rest of you!" she sobbed.

Her sisters sat uneasy around her. They felt superior to her, because they had not lost their spindles, but they also felt sorry for her. At length the second eldest spoke. "Why are we spinning at all?" she asked. "Who needs thread as fine as hens'-hair?" She gave a nudge with her foot, and pushed her spindle over the edge of the cloud. "There!" she said, and gasped at her own boldness. "Now I'm behind all of you, and I don't care!"

"Oh!" said the third sister. "How do you dare— well, I do too!" and she threw her own spindle, as far as she could throw. Creatures on the earth below saw it sail across the sky, a shooting star; and more, and more. Six shooting stars in all, one of them a little almost-dark star when Eldest Sister threw her spindle, for she had so little thread on it.

Eldest Sister's spindle stuck, standing straight up among the Wisstimandel Mountains, and there it is to this day. Someday, children, you may see it. The other sisters' spindles fell onto the earth, and nobody knows what became of them. But wherever the threads fell, trees sprang up tall, and among them monkeys and unicorns, phoenixes and griffins and dragonets. All the magical things and colors of the earth sprang up. These are the seven ley-lines, children. One day you may walk along them and see what magic the sisters dropped onto the earth when they threw away their spindles.

Up above, Great Light's daughters were no longer so happy. They had nothing to do, except regret their boldness. And what did they know how to do, except spin thread as fine as hens'-hair? Now they had said "Who needs thread as fine as hens'-hair?" and how was that any different from saying "Who needs us?" The only one of them who was contented was youngest sister, who lay with her face in a hole in the cloud, watching the wonders below. Monkeys and butterflies came to her hand, and she plucked fruit from the tallest branches of the trees.

"What shall we do when Father comes back?" said the second-youngest sister, one evening when the clouds were purple and gold. The sisters looked at each other and did not answer, for a while.

"I suppose we will go back into the sky," said Eldest Sister.

"And what will we do there? Nobody needs thread as fine as hens'-hair!"

"The earth needed it," said youngest sister. "Wherever it fell, the trees grew! Haven't you looked?"

Her sisters had not looked, that was true. Now they all lay down and put their faces through the clouds and marveled. "I will make some more," said Eldest Sister. "But I need my spindle!"

Youngest sister put her hand out, and a monkey brought her a twig with three green leaves. "Here is a spindle," she said to Eldest Sister, and Eldest Sister spun thread as green as springtime. One by one, the creatures brought new spindles to the eight sisters, and they spun

168

thread as gold as summer, as blue as winter, as scarlet as blood, as purple as crowsbill, as coral as the setting sun, as azure as the sea, and as rosy as the morning. As fast as they spun it, they cast it over the edge of their cloud onto the earth, and then put their faces through the clouds to see what wonders they had created.

Great Light came back one day and found his daughters all happily spinning, just as they should be. "I see you have been good girls while I was away," he said. But really, what had he to worry about? Because all they could do, those girls, was spin thread as fine as hens'-hair.

About the Author

"Great Light's Daughters" is a creation myth from Patricia S. Bowne's work in progress, *Fountain Girl*. More of Pat's short fiction can be found in magazines like Tales of the Unanticipated, Unsettling Wonder, Lorelei Signal, Rose Red Review, and in Year's Best Fantasy III; for novel readers, there's the Royal Academy at Osyth series from Double Dragon Press. Links to them all are at her website, www.raosyth.com.

*****~~~~*****

Abbreviated Epics

Qinggong Ji

by Stephen D. Rogers

At a time when peasants could not feed their own families, Ji was born an orphan.

In the beginning, she survived on the kindness of people who could not bear to see a child go hungry. She thanked them with her smile. As the years went by, Ji grew in strength and determination to remain free. She flitted in and out of villages, in and out of lives. As she approached the threshold of becoming a young woman, Ji vowed that her survival would benefit all those who needed her help.

At the height of one particular rainy season, Ji entered the Valley of Seven Echoes.

"What have we here?" A man armed with a sword spoke to her from inside a pavilion. "Is this a rat I see, come to steal our stores?"

Ji raised her face to the weather but said nothing.

"The rat doesn't speak."

"I was born in the year of the dragon."

"As was I, little one. What brings you here?"

"The wind and the lie of the land."

"And what do you want?"

"To repay your hospitality."

He bowed. "May I be the first to welcome you to our humble valley."

"The honor is mine." Ji lowered her head, tapped the ground ahead with her staff, and continued towards the village.

Parting the curtains of heavy rain as she walked, Ji wondered about the man standing guard in the pavilion. Against what was he posted to raise the alarm? A poet, perhaps, could find succor there alone on the edge of the valley, but Ji had not seen the tools of that particular trade.

A village that felt the need to protect itself in such weather could benefit from some kindness.

The peasants at the first house she reached brought her inside, gave her dry things to wear, and made her a bowl of tea. "Have you traveled far?"

"Warm in the pleasure of your company; I cannot imagine I ever left home." Ji set down her tea and unwrapped one of her two prized possessions, returning the soft fabrics to the bag she carried on her back. "If I may impose, I would ask that you grant me the opportunity to thank you as best I can."

After her hosts nodded, Ji placed the sound box of the erhu on her thigh, gripped the bow with her right hand, and rested the neck of the instrument in her left, positioning her fingers on the two strings.

She left her body and became part of everything.

Ji played a song that told the story of her life. Her audience wept at the hardships, cheered at her successes, and marveled at her bravery, for her story began with the love of her parents and ended with her love of all living things.

When she finished and apologized for her lack of skill, her hosts said that if her playing had not caused the rain to end and the sun to shine, it was only because of the severity of their surroundings.

Ji allowed each of the children to touch the erhu before she wrapped her instrument in its protective coverings. "Do you think the man in the pavilion would be offended by my song?"

"You should play first for the elder of the village."

"I hope he will not think me rude for not thinking of that myself."

Ji followed the family out into the rain, where they encountered other peasants who upon hearing Ji's music had gathered outside. Thus a crowd made its way to the largest house in the village, a crowd that grew as if new members sprouted from the damp soil.

The village elder ushered Ji into his home, and as many of the others crowded in as possible. The others waited outside in the rain.

After tea was distributed, Ji thanked the elder for his forbearance and asked whether he enjoyed the erhu.

After he confessed he did and begged her to honor him with her music, Ji once again played the song that told the story of her life.

Her audience wept at the hardships, cheered at her successes, and marveled at her bravery, for her story began with the love of her parents and ended with her love of all living things.

The village elder said he wished to thank Ji with a story of his own, the story of the village that lay within the Valley of the Seven Echoes.

Ji bid him continue.

The elder told of a beautiful village plagued by bandits that descended every rainy season.

Three men burst into the room and interrupted his story. The tallest with long dark hair spoke. "We are here, old man, to receive our due."

"The year has been a difficult one."

"That is not my concern. My concern is the hunger of my men."

Ji spoke without raising her head. "If you take everything the villagers have, they will be too weak to tend their crops. Next year when you come back, there will be no stores, and your men will go hungry, and the following year your men will be following someone else."

"You are a little girl who knows nothing of the world."

"I am the truth you are wise enough to recognize. This year you should eat elsewhere so that next year there will be enough."

"You are trouble." The bandit leader glared at the village elder. "We will return."

Peasants backed away from the men as they left.

Hoof beats grew softer.

The elder sighed. "You were both right. They will return, and we will starve."

"Then I must be ready with my instrument." Ji thanked her host and gathered herself. She set off into the rain and made her way up into the mountains that formed the valley.

She knew if three men could not convince the elder to release the village's bounty, then the bandits would return in force to take the stores by force.

Upon reaching a height that allowed her to watch the entrance to the valley and also the mountains in case the bandits knew of a pass, Ji sat on her haunches and became one with the crags.

While the heavy rain limited visibility, the weather would also slow the bandits, might even change the strategies with which they were familiar.

There they were, forty men on horses trudging through the rain-swept entrance to the valley. The armed man from the pavilion went out to challenge them. Five dismounted and defeated him.

As the bandits continued towards the village, Ji laid her staff aside and carefully unwrapped her instrument. The bandits were now deep within the valley.

Ji ran along the mountaintops, playing the erhu as she flew from edge to outcropping. She strummed and plucked the strings to make sounds of men, of horses, of canon being moved into position.

She wove the story of an army preparing to strike.

As Ji leapt up rock and down cliff along the mountains that ringed the valley and back, her erhu produced long looping lines of attackers above the bandits.

Dizzy with fear, the bandits whipped themselves into a storm-tossed frenzy, until they ignored their leader's shouts and broke, horses sliding on the slippery ground. The bandits fled in fear of being completely surrounded.

The valley was once again visited only by rain that fell in long, flowing ribbons.

Ji allowed the final vibrations of the erhu strings to die before she rewrapped her instrument. After recovering her staff, she descended to the village, where the illusion she'd created still echoed.

The villagers stood in the downpour to greet and thank Ji for saving them. The elder gathered the children and whispered to their leader, a thin boy of indeterminate age. The children spoke among themselves and then created a dance to recall Ji's exploits on their behalf.

Ji applauded their efforts, not because they glorified her, but because the dance would serve to remind the children how to face and overcome dangerous challenges, would stand as a lesson that could be passed down.

She bowed to them. "You have paid me a great honor."

The glow of the crowd dimmed at the sound of thunder.

Rolling thunder. Thunder that increased in volume and intensity, echoing off the mountains.

Ji opened the bag containing the erhu and put the instrument aside in a sheltered place. Gripping the second of her prized possessions, her staff, she turned to face the entrance to the valley.

The mounted bandits raced towards the village at breakneck speed.

The villagers scattered.

Ji swung the staff in a large arc and only stopped when the weapon hung balanced above her head.

She had used reason, and she had used imagination, but the bandits would not listen. She would now speak to them in a new language by using their advantages against them.

Ji focused her eyes to see everything: the men and their plans, the horses and their desires, the dark sky and falling rain and slippery land. She saw the obstacles of buildings, fences, and trees. She saw the potential of rocks and tools and barrels. She saw in all directions of space and time.

She became one with the all.

The bandits reached her.

Ji swung her staff and thrust, separating this horse from its hoofs, that rider from his horse, this weapon from its owner.

She deflected and dodged blows, moving fast enough to slide through raindrops. Though vastly outnumbered, she could not be overwhelmed, because she never remained in any single place long enough for her enemies to converge on her.

The bandits gradually lost their momentum, their attack dissolving in the rain.

Ji continued to spin and flip. She ran up walls to fly through the air. She planted her staff to power her kicks. She appeared out of nowhere and everywhere.

The bandits staggered about, confused and dispirited. Their heavier weapons tired their muscles and upset their balance.

Ji pressed her attack, harassing her enemy with strikes from all directions.

First one and then more of the village children joined the fray, taunting the bandits and pelting them with rocks. Some of the children grabbed rakes and spades to trip the invaders. Others jumped on backs and pulled hair.

Adults called from doorways and windows. Then they shouted from outside their homes. Then they stood beside their children, which allowed them to change their fear into rage.

As the men and women of the village entered the battle, Ji concentrated on the leader of the bandits, isolating him from the rest of his band.

She swung and thrust and knocked him to the ground. Knelt next to him in the mud, pinning the staff against his windpipe.

"You will never visit this village again. You will prove your ability to lead by taking your men elsewhere and presenting them with richer pickings that give them less trouble. Grunt if you understand me."

He grunted.

"You have an opportunity. From what I hear, this village doesn't produce enough to reliably feed your band. If you don't go elsewhere, you're risking your position as head of your band." Ji let up on his neck. "Do the smart thing and move on."

Again, he grunted.

Ji stood, allowing him to climb to his feet.

He rubbed his throat. "You are nothing but a little girl."

"I am. And you should go quickly, before your men realize that you did not win."

The man collected his band and led them out of the valley, the rain covering the sound of their retreat and then hiding them from sight.

Ji thanked the villagers for saving her. She partook in the celebratory feast, admired the children's new dance that recalled the exploits of their families, and ended the evening by unwrapping her erhu and playing her song.

The next morning Ji rose early, apologized to her hosts for imposing on their hospitality, and set off into the rain, forever leaving behind the village nestled within the Valley of Seven Echoes.

About the Author

Stephen D. Rogers is the author of *A DICTIONARY OF MADE-UP LANGUAGES* and more than 800 shorter pieces. His website, www.StephenDRogers.com, includes a list of new and upcoming titles as well as other timely information.

*****~~~~*****

On a Train With a Coyote Ghost

by Robin Wyatt Dunn

Inspired by a painting with the same title, by Barbara Sobczyńska

I am heading east, into Kursk.

The coyote ghost is coming too.

It is snowing.

I am not afraid of the coyote ghost; I like him. He is very large.

Outside it is very cold, and growing colder.

I am going to see The Worker. I need broth for my grandmother. Her village has been ill, my grandmother especially. This is why I am going to Kursk, where The Worker is said to live now. My papers have been prepared; they are in my purse. My mother bought me the purse; it is black, like my hair.

I am not afraid, because the coyote ghost is with me; he is my father's. For years, he was my father's friend. Now he is coming with me, over the border, on the train.

My name is Jezebel, and I am a Jew. But inside, I am more ancient.

I do not know how old I am, inside. Outside, I am ten.

…

When my father was in the army, he met the coyote ghost in a bombed village, outside of Beograd. My father, who was good with animals because he was a hunter, asked the coyote ghost what he was doing in a village outside Beograd, since coyotes only occur in the Americas.

"I am a ghost and can live wherever I please," the coyote ghost told him.

"You should leave here; there are more dogs where I live."

179

"Where do you live?" asked the coyote ghost.

"Krakow."

That is how I met the coyote ghost; he came home with my father, after the Americans bombed Serbia.

Long ago, The Worker's ancestors crossed over the Bering Strait into the Americas, taking our traditions with them. Now, one of them has returned, as a ghost.

...

I know that the coyote ghost sometimes thinks about eating me. This is in its nature. I do not think about eating the coyote; it is a ghost. Also, I do not care to eat dogs.

The coyote ghost is coming with me to help me at the border.

...

It is night, but soon it will be morning. Every hour, the conductor walks through my car, to see that everything is in order. I am the only passenger in this car. People are poor now, and my mother saved for a long time to buy me this ticket. When the conductor passes through, I hide the coyote ghost under my purse. Because he is a coyote, he is very good at hiding in tight places, although he is many times my size.

"When you understand the intentions of the Russians, you will know that you are passing into a liminal space within the mind which is defined by color, and shape, and movement," the coyote ghost is saying, staring into my eyes. "I cannot tell you in advance what they will do. But once you understand what they are going to do, you will understand what your own actions must be, to satisfy the needs of the gate at the Russian border. Even in life, coyotes must be cognizant of gates, and in death, more so. If the Russian guards are going to refuse you, you will know in advance, if you pay attention. If they refuse you, I will take one action. If they admit you, I will take another. Do you understand?"

"Of course," I said. "But what will you do if they refuse me?"

"That is for me to know," the coyote said. "Naturally, you could always give up now and let me eat you."

"Not just yet," I said. "Maybe later."

"Hmm," said the coyote

...

Our ancestors were great students of Nature, especially plants. The Worker knows which plants can be used for special purposes, such as divination. My grandmother is a powerful visionary, but even her talents she says are not enough for what we are facing now, and so I have been chosen to go and get the broth, because it is needed.

I am not afraid.

The coyote holds my hand, in its paw, and slowly, I fall asleep, with the snow outside, and the train humming beneath my body.

...

When I awake, it is already morning. We are approaching the border. The conductor enters the car, and the coyote ghost hides under my purse.

"Not there," I whisper to him, and he hides instead under my skirt.

I pick up my purse and take out my papers to show to the conductor.

"Good morning, *dzyevushka*. Papers, please."

I hand him my papers. He examines them carefully. Then he places his stamp on them.

"Who is meeting you in Kursk?" he asks.

"My father," I tell him. But my father is dead.

The conductor notes this in his notebook, then leaves. Outside, I can see the city in the dawn light.

"You can come out now," I tell the coyote ghost. He comes out from under my skirt.

"They will let me in," I say.

181

"Don't be so sure," says the coyote ghost.

A hundred meters from the edge of the city, the train screeches to a halt.

"Open the window," says the coyote ghost.

I am afraid. And the window is stuck. I pound on it with my fist.

"Open it," says the coyote.

I pound and pound on it; I can hear men coming in the next car. My hand is bleeding. Finally it opens, and freezing air swirls into the car, filled with snowflakes and yellow-red light.

The coyote pushes me out the window, and I land in the snow beside the tracks.

"What will you do?" I shout at the coyote ghost.

"Now you run," he says, looking at me from the window with his strange eyes.

I am running through the snow. Behind me I can hear soldiers.

"Halt!" one of the soldiers shouts, in Russian.

I run faster.

Behind me, I can hear the coyote, and I look back; he is much larger than the train, glowing in the dawn light, his smile terrible, and gleaming, and I scream at him not to kill them, but I look away.

I do not know if he killed them or not.

I am in the woods. I am crying, under a tree. I still have my purse my mother bought me. Inside it is the letter to The Worker.

...

I do not hear anything after ten minutes, and so as not to freeze I get up and walk, towards Kursk.

...

I believe the coyote understands the sickness in my grandmother's village, but he will not tell me what the sickness is.

I am walking. The sun is climbing. My hand hurts. My feet are very cold in the snow.

On a Train With a Coyote Ghost

In the distance, the train is still standing there, motionless. I walk, staying under the trees, until I find myself in someone's back garden.

I have made it. I am in Russia. I must find The Worker's address. The shaman.

...

An old woman invites me into her house for tea, and I don't speak very much Russian, so I just nod, and smile. She is talking about her son, who died in the war. Which war, I don't know. She is very old, as old as my grandmother.

I show her the address I have written down.

"*Gdje*?" I ask her. "Where?"

She draws me a map, with a pencil she sharpens with her knife.

...

Kursk is smaller than Krakow, and lonelier. I walk towards the center of town, but most people do not meet my eye. I am afraid of soldiers, but they do not look at me either.

I can feel the coyote ghost close by, but I do not see him.

Outside the Church of the Ascension, playing in the mushroom fountain, I see The Worker. I know it is him. His address is still five blocks away but I know this is him. He is singing to himself, and washing himself in the church fountain.

I walk to him immediately and say, "Mr. Worker?"

He smiles at me. He keeps singing and washing himself.

"Mr. Worker? Is it you?"

"I am washing," he says, smiling at me.

"I am sorry to interrupt your bath. My name is Jezebel. I need your help."

"You are a Jew," he says.

"Yes," I say.

"I am a Jew too," he says, smiling.

"You are?"

"Also, I am a Buddhist."

"I see."

"Here, come take a bath with me," he says.

"No, thank you," I say. "I will wait till you are done."

"I'm almost done," he says.

Mass has started inside the church, and I can hear the priest singing. The snow has slowed; I stand under the eaves of the church, to stay warm.

"It is warmer in the water!" the Worker shouts, laughing.

I try to smile, but my teeth are chattering too hard. I wonder where the coyote is.

Finally The Worker finishes his bath, and he pops a small mushroom in his mouth, while wrapping a towel around his body.

"Come with me," he says, and he starts to climb up the rain gutter on the side of the church.

"Is it okay?" I ask.

"Yes, come on!"

It's better to move than stand still in this cold, so I grab ahold of the rain gutter and dig my feet into the side of the church and start to climb up.

The Worker reaches the edge of the big blue dome at the top of the church.

"We shouldn't be up here!" I whisper to him.

"It's fine, you're only a little girl, and I'm only a little man! Come on!"

I follow him into the dome, stepping very carefully, holding out my hands for balance. My purse, with the letter inside it, is hanging around my neck. Somewhere, in the clouds above, I can feel the coyote.

The Worker lifts the cross on top of the dome like a hatch, and it opens just like a door. I am amazed, and the Worker smiles at me. Inside the dome is his little hut, just like our ancestors had.

On a Train With a Coyote Ghost

"Come on in," he says, and I do. I climb down the ladder and sit down by his fire, and then I see that the coyote is already here.

"I see you've brought my old friend The Wolf!" says The Worker.

"He is a coyote," I say, and coyote smiles.

"Same difference!" says The Worker. "Will you have tea?"

"I'm not supposed to do any drugs," I tell The Worker.

"This is just tea!"

"Okay," I say, and The Worker pours tea for the three of us.

It tastes delicious. It tastes like the forest.

…

Part of me is afraid The Worker put drugs in the tea anyway, but I know that I'm tired, and only a little while ago I was running from Russian soldiers. The Worker seems to expand and contract like a balloon, but I tell myself that it's okay, and soon he will give me the broth I need to take to my grandmother.

…

The coyote ghost and The Worker had a lot to talk about; it was clear they were old friends. I tried to listen, but I couldn't understand a lot of it. Mostly about history, and wars, and adventures they had had together, and old arguments.

Then I heard the coyote ghost tell The Worker, "She isn't worthy of your potion. Give it to me instead, so I can bring it to my family in America. We need it more than this little Pole." I gasped.

The Worker smiled. "Are you willing to fight for your little broth, Jezebel?"

"Yes," I said, and swallowed.

"How shall you fight?" asked The Worker.

"By hook or by crook," said the coyote, smiling.

"With stories," I said.

The Worker smiled. "I like that idea," he said. "Each of you tell me a story. If I don't like either of them, I can always eat both of you. Coyote, you go first, you're older."

Coyote began his story.

...

"I have been hungry for a long time," said the coyote, "longer than either of you have been alive. When I was a little pup, I hungered for human flesh, and now that I am dead, I hunger for it more. It has been so long since I had any. Before I took a wife, I found a boy outside Phoenix. In Arizona the Americans were killing many Mexicans, and they had left a boy outside near a cactus, and he was very tired, because he had been running from the soldiers. I killed him and ate him there, and it was the best thing I had ever tasted. The boy tasted like fear, and like love, and like memory, which is, I later realized, what my wife tasted like too.

"Because I had eaten that boy, I grew a hunger for humans, and looked for ways to eat another. But the war had ended, and human flesh became much harder to come by. I longed for someone to leave a small child unattended, or a baby abandoned, but found nothing.

"Still I could not forget my hunger. It burned in me, like a fuel, and even after I had gotten married and fathered children I would spend many hours alone, on the edges of Phoenix, looking for a human to eat. All I found was cactus, and the occasional rabbit.

"When I realized I could not forget about my hunger no matter how much I tried, I prayed to the Old Gods of the Dogs, They Who Howl, and sacrificed some of my blood into the river water, one summer. Then I had a vision of what I was to do. I was to kill my son with my own teeth, They Who Howl told me, and then I would be given a human to eat, at my leisure.

186

On a Train With a Coyote Ghost

"Possessed with the vision, I sought out my son, who was now grown, and who had moved to Los Angeles, where he lived in the arroyo, with his cousin.

"All over Los Angeles I prowled, seeking my own flesh, so I could propitiate the will of my gods. At last I found him in his arroyo, but I saw that he was now stronger than me. And he saw my intentions in my eyes, and he and his cousin beat me, and drove me from the arroyo limping, into the city, where I dodged cars, and ran from children who taunted me, wondering where was my desert, and where were my gods, and where was my wife, and where was I, but there was only asphalt, not even any stars to navigate by.

"I died there in Los Angeles, lost and alone. Shortly after I died, I was given a choice. I could serve my family as a ghost, as compensation for my abandonment and madness, or I could be reincarnated as a human being. Reincarnation I found disgusting, and so I chose the first option.

"It was a good choice, because I had to learn a lot to become a proper servant of The Coyotes. I had thought myself a well educated canid, but I knew almost nothing in life. In death, I learned what diplomacy was, and what war is. I learned to speak human tongues, and I traveled widely, including to Serbia, where I met this girl's father.

"When I met Jezebel, she made me remember my own son, and my foolish promise to the gods. That is why I agreed to help her help her family. But on the train, something occurred to me. This sickness has afflicted all of us, for many generations. Why should it be this little Polish family that gets to receive the cure from your wise hands, Worker? Why not give it to The Coyotes? Have we not served you longer, with more loyalty in our disloyalty, and more trickery in our loyal hearts even as your loyalty is trickery in the ways of your awesome magic? Hasn't my family earned your cure for our affliction, these many years?

"On the train I realized that this girl is too over-eager. She believes too easily. She thinks that I would help her simply because I was a friend of her father's. But she forgets that I am a coyote. And I hunger, even now, for human flesh. Give me the potion, Worker, and let me eat her, and before I crumble into dust and cease to be forever, I will be your coyote, and work your great will wherever you say."

The coyote smiled his great toothy smile, and I could not look at him, I hated him so much. So I began my story, speaking in as loud a voice as I could.

"My name is Jezebel, and I am a Jew. I am ten years old. My grandmother is dying. So is my grandmother's village. For five hundred years my people have lived here in Poland, and before that, we lived for five thousand years in Israel, the land of Sarah's God. Before that, we lived with you, Worker, in Egypt, and south of Egypt, in Africa. Before I was a Jew, I was a girl, and before I was a girl, I was a human being, and before I was a human being, I was a mammal, like you, Worker, and like you, coyote, cut from flesh on my mother's umbilical cord, and like coyote, I want to help my family.

"Although we are Jews, my grandmother remembers the older ways, Worker, which is why she knew where you lived. I know that Coyote suffered a great deal, and that humans treated him poorly. And I can't promise to serve you as the coyote has; I am not a ghost, and I must serve my family.

"But I think that if you give me your magic broth, Worker, and let me give it to my grandmother, she will share it with her whole village, and her village is very strong, Worker, and they will learn to make more of your magic broth, and we will share it with as many people as we can."

I swallowed. I couldn't think of anything else to say.

"So. . . you're offering to put me out of business!" The Worker laughed. "Ha ha ha ha! I like it! You win, girly! The broth is yours!"

And with that, the coyote snarled, and disappeared into a mist, out into the night.

…

Getting back to Krakow was not as easy as it was to leave it. It took me almost a year.

Sometimes I still dream about the coyote.

Now, in Krakow, we have begun to manufacture the broth that cured my grandmother's village. Even in America they are buying it. I hope some of it gets to the coyote's family, in Phoenix.

I know that he meant well, though he had an evil smile.

About the Author

Robin Wyatt Dunn has lived in his adopted state of California longer than anywhere else. This year he started teaching composition in colleges in Los Angeles. His new novel is *A Map of Kex's Face*, due out at the end of the year. More information is at robindunn.com/kex.html. Check out his website for a list of his published books, stories, and poems.

*****~~~~~*****

Credits and Acknowledgments

Cover image and design – Keely Rew

Illustrations (ebook only)
HMS Invisible and the Halifax Slaver – U.S. brig *Perry* [confronting] American slave ship *Martha* off Ambriz June 6, 1850. Wikimedia Commons, U.S. Navy History Center website, Commander Andrew H. Foote, author, *Africa and the American Flag*.

Assault on the Summit – Sir Edmund Hilary statue over Himalayas. Creative Commons via Flickr. Uploaded by user: Schwede66

Damfino Plays for Table Stakes – Poker chips. Creative Commons license. Uploaded by Jamie Adams from Hull, United Kingdom

Fortunate Son – Reconstruction drawing of the woman who owned the Klinta Staff. From Vikingar exhibition at Swedish History Museum. Drawing: Mats Vänehem. Uploaded by user: Lotta Fernstål

The Perfection of the Steam-Powered Armour – Samurai helmet, about 1550, and half-face mask (menpo), Japan. Ann and Gabriel Barbier-Mueller Museum, Dallas, Texas; photograph taken during an exhibition in the Musée des Arts Premiers in Paris. Commons.wikimedia.org, author: Vassil.

Odin on the Tree – Illustration to Baldr's Draumar, "Odin Rides to Hel." Painting by W.G. Collingwood, 1908. Commons.wikimedia.org, public domain.

The Lost Children – Bull fresco on north entrance of the Minoan palace of Knossos. Children who may have been sacrificed were found at the site. User: Deror avi/Crete.

On a Train With a Coyote Ghost – painting by Barbara Sobczyńska, used by permission.

Readers

Andrew Cairns, Tom Parker, Keely Rew

*****~~~~*****

Discover other titles by Third Flatiron:

(1) Over the Brink: Tales of Environmental Disaster

(2) A High Shrill Thump: War Stories

(3) Origins: Colliding Causalities

(4) Universe Horribilis

(5) Playing with Fire

(6) Lost Worlds, Retraced

(7) Redshifted: Martian Stories

(8) Astronomical Odds

(9) Master Minds

www.thirdflatiron.com

THIRD FLATIRON